"Why didn't you keep in touch? Or maybe even come back in the summer?"

Chloe shook her head, hating to admit the truth for fear of just how silly this all was. One kiss. She'd lived off it all these years because it had been so perfect. At least in her memory. "I was afraid."

"Afraid?"

"Afraid it wasn't anything. That maybe I misread the kiss, that..." She shrugged again as she looked into his handsome face. This cowboy had been in her dreams for years, and now here he was in the flesh. Could real life live up to the fantasy Justin Calhoun? She thought it just might.

"Do you even remember the kiss?"

He held her gaze. "What do you think?"

She swallowed again and had to look away. "We were so young."

"You think that makes a difference?"

"I don't know." She turned back to him. "What do you think?"

"That we might have to test it."

RUGGED DEFENDER

New York Times Bestselling Author
B.J. DANIELS

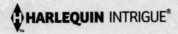

This book is for Lu Besel, one of the most gracious women I know. I want to be you when I grow up.

ISBN-13: 978-1-335-52670-0

Rugged Defender

Copyright © 2018 by Barbara Heinlein

Recycling programs
for this product may
not exist in your area.

Printed in U.S.A.

www.Harlequin.com

B.J. Daniels is a *New York Times* and *USA TODAY* bestselling author. She wrote her first book after a career as an award-winning newspaper journalist and author of thirty-seven published short stories. She lives in Montana with her husband, Parker, and three springer spaniels. When not writing, she quilts, boats and plays tennis. Contact her at bjdaniels.com, on Facebook or on Twitter, @bjdanielsauthor.

Books by B.J. Daniels

Harlequin Intrigue

Whitehorse, Montana: The Clementine Sisters

Hard Rustler
Rogue Gunslinger
Rugged Defender

The Montana Cahills

Cowboy's Redemption

Whitehorse, Montana: The McGraw Kidnapping

Dark Horse
Dead Ringer
Rough Rider

HQN Books

The Montana Cahills

Renegade's Pride
Outlaw's Honor
Hero's Return
Rancher's Dream

Visit the Author Profile page at Harlequin.com.

CAST OF CHARACTERS

Justin Calhoun—The son of a wealthy rancher returns to Whitehorse to find out if he was right about one magical winter kiss years ago—and to solve a murder.

Chloe Clementine—The investigative reporter can't resist a mystery—especially when it involves a man she's never forgotten after one magical winter kiss years ago.

Bert Calhoun—He lost his favorite son. But what is killing him is that he believes his only other son was the murderer.

Drew Calhoun—His death was ruled accidental, but no one believes that, especially his father. The problem is that a lot of people wanted Drew dead.

Nicole "Niki" Kent—She knew both Calhoun men. One she loved. The other she hated. And she was there the night Drew died.

Pete Ferris—The insurance man had reason to want Drew Calhoun dead after Drew befriended Pete's wife.

Monte Decker—The banker had been cheated by Drew in a poker game, but did he hate Drew enough to kill him?

Patsy Carter Simpson—She knew Drew as well as anyone. It's why she broke up with him and married someone else.

Blaine Simpson—The big cowboy just wanted Drew to leave his wife alone.

Thad Zimmerman—The Calhoun ranch manager had his own reasons for wanting the youngest son to stay gone.

CJ Hanson—He wanted his best friend's killer to pay. But then again, he was a bully who wanted everyone to pay.

Emily Ferris—Pete's wife might have been the only person in town who saw another side to Drew Calhoun. Or she might have killed him.

Chapter One

It all began with a kiss. At least that's the way Chloe Clementine remembered it. A winter kiss, which is nothing like a summer one. The cold, icy air around you. Puffs of white breaths intermingling. Warm lips touching, tingling as they meet for the very first time.

Chloe thought that kiss would be the last thing she remembered before she died of old age. It was the kiss—and the cowboy who'd kissed her—that she'd been dreaming about when her phone rang. Being in Whitehorse had brought it all back after all these years.

She groaned, wanting to keep sleeping so she could stay in that cherished memory longer. Her phone rang again. She swore that if it was one of her sisters calling this early...

"What?" she demanded into the phone without bothering to see who was calling. She'd been so sure that it would be her youngest sister, Annabelle, the morning person.

"Hello?" The voice was male and familiar. For just a moment she thought she'd conjured up the cowboy from the kiss. "It's Justin."

Justin? She sat straight up in bed. Thoughts zipped past at a hundred miles an hour. How had he gotten her cell phone number? Why was he calling? Was he in Whitehorse?

"Justin," she said, her voice sounding croaky from sleep. She cleared her throat. "I thought it was Annabelle calling. What's up?" She glanced at the clock. What's up at seven forty-five in the morning?

"I know it's early but I got your message."

Now she really was confused. "My message?" She had danced with his best friend at the Christmas Dance recently, but she hadn't sent Justin a message.

"That you needed to see me? That it was urgent?"

She had no idea what he was talking about. Had her sister Annabelle done this? She couldn't imagine her sister Tessa Jane "TJ" doing such a thing. But since her sisters had fallen in love they hadn't been themselves.

"I'm sorry, but I didn't send you a message. You're sure it was from me?"

"The person calling just told me that you were in trouble and needed my help. There was loud music in the background as if whoever it was might have called me from a bar."

He didn't think she'd drunk-dialed him, did he? "Sorry, but it wasn't me." She was more sorry than he knew. "And I can't imagine who would have called you on my behalf." Like the devil, she couldn't. It had to be her sister Annabelle.

"Well, I'm glad to hear that you aren't in trouble and urgently need my help," he said, not sounding like that at all.

She closed her eyes, now wishing she'd made something up. *What was she thinking?* She didn't need to improvise. She *was* in trouble, though nothing urgent exactly. At least for the moment. And since she hadn't told anyone about what was going on with her...

"Are you in Whitehorse?" she asked.

"No. I haven't been back for years." There was regret in his voice that made her think he hadn't left because he wanted to. Odd.

"Me either. I came home to be with my sisters for the holidays. I appreciate you calling though. It's nice to know that if I was in trouble, you'd..." He hadn't exactly said that he'd come running. "Call. It's good to hear your voice."

"Yours too. It's been a long time."

Too long. She wondered if he ever thought of her—and their kiss. Her sisters referred to Justin T. Calhoun as her high school boyfriend. But in truth, they'd barely gotten together before she'd had to leave for college. There'd just been that snowy-day kiss. He'd gone on to reportedly get engaged to Nicole "Nici" Kent, break up, and then get married to and divorced from Margie Taylor while Chloe had been busy getting her journalism degree and working her way up from one newspaper to another larger one.

While she'd dated some, none of the men she'd met stood up to what she called The Kiss Test. None of them had come close to Justin's winter kiss.

"So how long are you staying in Whitehorse?" he asked, dragging her from her thoughts.

"Until the first." The truth was, her plans after that were rather up in the air. Not even her sisters knew the real story. "Maybe longer."

"So you'll be there for the New Year's Eve Masquerade Dance."

It was only days away. Annabelle had been trying to talk her into going but Chloe had been adamant that she wasn't. Her sisters had dragged her to the Christmas Dance and that was bad enough. Nothing could change her mind… Except Justin.

She hedged. "I haven't made up my mind yet about going. Are you thinking about it?" she asked hopefully.

He laughed. "You and I never got a chance to dance."

They'd never gotten a chance to do a lot of things. "No," she said. "You dance?"

He chuckled. "You'd have to be the judge of that. Maybe I'll see you there. It's been nice talking with you, Chloe. You take care." And he was gone.

"Maybe I'll see you there"? Not, "I'll see you there"? Not, "let's make it a date and I'll come back to Whitehorse"? But still her heart was a hammer in her chest. Just the thought of seeing Justin again…

She told herself that it had been years. He might have changed. The chemistry might not even be there anymore. How could she even be sure it had been there to start with? It had been just one kiss.

The doorbell rang, followed by the front door opening and excited voices. Moments later, she heard noisy chatter on the stairs. Chloe wanted to put her head back under the covers.

"I bet she's not even up yet," she heard TJ say.

"Well, we'd better wake her up otherwise we're going to be late."

Chloe didn't like the sound of this. Before she could move, her sisters burst into her bedroom.

"Get up, sleepyhead," Annabelle said. "We have a surprise for you."

She didn't like surprises and said as much. Also she suspected she'd already gotten one of her sisters' surprises this morning.

"Annabelle volunteered us to work at the local soup kitchen today just like we did as kids," TJ told her. It had been one of their grandmother's pet projects. When their parents were killed in a car wreck, the three of them had moved to Whitehorse, Montana, to live with the grandmother they'd never met. Grandma Frannie was gone now, but she'd left Annabelle her house a few months ago, which their sister had readied for them for the holidays.

"It will make you a better person," TJ said, sounding enough like their grandmother that Chloe had to laugh.

"Fine. Let me get dressed." She watched her sisters start to leave. "Justin just called me."

They both froze before turning to face her. "Seriously?" Annabelle said, clearly trying to keep her face straight. "What did he say?"

"That someone had called him from a bar telling him I was in trouble and that it was urgent. The person apparently gave him my cell phone number." She looked from one sister to the next and back. "I know it was you, Annabelle."

Her sister laughed. "Wrong."

"It was Annabelle's idea," TJ said quickly. "But I made the call. Too much wine. I'm sorry. Guess you should have come to the bar with us the other night."

She wanted to scold them both but could only shake her head.

"So how did the call go?" Annabelle asked, looking excited.

"He said he might see me at the Masquerade Dance."

"Really? That's great!" Annabelle exchanged a high five with TJ. "I told you it would work."

"It didn't work. It's not like he promised to come back to Whitehorse or attend the dance. He said maybe." She could see that this didn't dampen either of her sisters' spirits or their belief that their call was successful.

"Oh, I hope he comes," Annabelle said. "It's so sad. I'm sure his friend Cooper told you."

"Told me what?"

"Justin's older brother, Drew. He was killed. Justin found him."

Drew had already been out of high school by the time Chloe was a freshman, so she'd never really known him. "That's horrible," Chloe said and saw from her sister's expression that there was more. "What?"

"It happened five years ago. Drew's death was ruled an accident but…" She looked at TJ.

"But what?" Chloe asked.

"Justin was under suspicion," Annabelle said. Since returning home to Whitehorse, her youngest sister had gotten caught up on all the local gossip thanks to a bunch of nosy elderly neighbors. "No one who knew him thought he'd been involved, but his father…well, I guess he still blames Justin."

Chloe couldn't believe what she was hearing. "Poor Justin. I had no idea. So much tragedy. Why would his father blame him?"

Annabelle shrugged. "Apparently Bert Calhoun idolized his oldest son. Justin and Drew were often at odds. That day Drew and Justin had an argument. That's all I know except that Justin left town and hasn't come back. We'd better get going or we're going to be late."

TJ had picked up a newspaper that Chloe had left on a table by the bedroom door, before saying,

"I'm surprised you were able to get so much time off from the paper. So you're staying until after the New Year, right?"

"I thought we were going to be late?" Chloe said. "Let me get showered and dressed." She shooed them out, but she could tell that TJ wasn't going to let the subject drop. At some point, Chloe knew she would have to tell them the truth.

JUSTIN T. CALHOUN leaned back, his boots resting on the large pine stump he used for a footstool, and thought about the phone call. Just hearing Chloe's voice had brought back the few sweet memories he had of Whitehorse. After everything that had happened, was it any wonder he'd been glad to leave it all behind?

But jumping feetfirst into a marriage to Margie Taylor had been a mistake, he thought as he looked out at the flat, white landscape of North Dakota. He could admit now that he'd been trying to put everything behind him. He'd worked her family ranch during their very short marriage. It hadn't taken Margie long to realize that his heart wasn't in it. Not in her or ranching her family's place. They'd parted as friends and he'd gone to work for another rancher near the Montana–North Dakota border. He hadn't even considered going home.

And yet the moment he'd heard Chloe Clementine was in trouble, he'd been ready to jump on his trusty steed and ride off to save her. He hadn't been that man in years and yet, instantly, he'd wanted to be. Because as much as he tried to fool himself, he had unfinished business in Whitehorse.

He stretched out his long denim-clad legs and looked around the small cabin he'd called home for months. It kept the snow out, but that was about all he could say about it. He didn't mind living modestly. Or at least he never had.

Talking to Chloe had left him restless. It reminded him that once, a long time ago, he'd had dreams. It also made him think about what he'd given up all those years ago. Is this what it took to get him to finally face the past? He thought about their kiss on that winter night, just the two of them with ice crystals floating around them.

"You damn fool," he said to himself and yet he couldn't help smiling. He'd always wanted to go to the New Year's Eve Masquerade Dance in Whitehorse. The idea of showing up and surprising Chloe... Just the thought of seeing her again...

At the sound of a truck approaching, he cursed and stood. He had someone else's cattle to feed, someone else's fence to mend. He shoved his worn Stetson down on his head, aware that he needed a haircut. A shave wouldn't hurt either. But what was the point of even thinking about making a change— let alone trying to go back to what could have been? Chloe didn't need him. So why had he said that he might show up at the party?

Worse, why was he thinking it was time to make things right?

AT THE EDGE of town, the wind whipped the new snow, swirling it around the empty cemetery. The huge old pine trees creaked and swayed. His tracks filled behind him as Bert Calhoun made his way to the granite tombstone.

He hated this trek through the cemetery each year. He knew he should come more often, but it was too painful. He felt old, forgotten, his heart as bleak as the winter landscape around him.

His footsteps faltered as he neared his oldest son's final resting place. A large pine stood like a sentinel over the grave. He read what had been carved into the granite as if the words were carved into his own flesh.

Andrew "Drew" Calhoun
July 4, 1982–December 10, 2013

Bert Calhoun removed his Stetson and squatted down next to the grave, his bad knee aching. The wind whipped at his too-long gray hair and beard. He was glad he was alone on this cold winter day. He kept to the ranch except when forced to come in for supplies. He knew people talked about him. They stared and whispered when they saw him. He could well imagine what they said.

Other than this yearly visit, he couldn't bring himself to even drive by the cemetery. He never knew what to say to his son. Drew had had so much promise from the time he was born. He was the one Bert had always depended on to take over the ranch and keep the Calhoun name and brand going.

That Drew had been taken from them so soon was still dynamite to his heart. There'd been days when he thought he couldn't go on breathing at the thought of his oldest son under six feet of dirt. Had there been anyone else to take over the ranch, he would have blessedly taken his own life. Instead, the circumstances of his son's death had him dying slowly from the pain. It had made him into a tired, bitter old man.

The wind whipped snow past, rocking the metal container holding the faded plastic flowers on the grave next to Drew's. He looked over at the headstone and felt the weight of his guilt. Pushing to his feet, he moved to his wife's graveside.

Mary Harris Calhoun
May 11, 1954–December 21, 2002

Losing her so young had made him hold on even tighter to Drew, since Drew resembled her the most. Now he was just glad she hadn't been around to see what had become of the family she'd loved so much. He knew how disappointed she would be in him. No more than he was in himself.

The promise was on his lips, but he couldn't bring himself to voice it. It wasn't the promise Mary would have wanted to hear. But it was the promise he'd made since Drew's murder five years ago this month. He would see that their oldest son's killer was brought to justice—one way or another.

But he hadn't been able to do even that.

The promise Mary wanted was one he couldn't even bring himself to utter let alone make happen even for her. Each time he came here, he could hear her as if she spoke from the grave.

Bring our son home. Make amends for what you've done.

Just the thought of his youngest son, Justin, doubled him over. When he closed his eyes, he saw Justin standing over his brother, the gun in his hand.

Hot tears ran down his cheeks. He felt even more guilt because his tears were for himself, and Mary knew it. From her grave, she blamed him as if he was the one who had pulled the trigger and ended Drew's life.

He shook his head. He wanted justice like his next breath. But some days he wasn't sure what justice would look like. Maybe he was already getting it and this was his punishment for the mistakes he'd made.

And yet he couldn't let go of what he felt in his heart. Justin had killed his brother. It felt like the truth, one that ate at him, fueled by his grief and his guilt.

He brushed at his tears now freezing to his cheeks and rose. He didn't need Mary to tell him the part he'd played in this tragedy. He'd always loved Drew more and everyone knew it—including Justin. And this was the price he paid.

No, not even after five years could he promise Mary that he would make things right with Justin. Not as long as he believed his youngest son was a killer.

Chapter Two

The moment they walked into the local soup kitchen, Chloe spotted Nicole Kent and groaned. "What is she doing here?" she whispered to her sisters.

"Apparently arguing with Edna," Annabelle said. "Edna Kirkland is the kitchen supervisor. Do not argue with her."

Chloe had no desire to argue with anyone, especially the large woman who was towering over Justin's old girlfriend, Nici.

Nici held up what appeared to be a hairnet and said in a strident voice, "I'm not wearing this." She was still short and cute in a rough sort of way with dyed black hair cut in a pixie that suited her.

Edna crossed her arms over her abundant chest and narrowed her eyes. "You'll wear it or I'll call the sheriff and have you thrown in jail." She smiled. "Your choice. Community service or jail. Those are your only options."

"No one mentioned I had to wear a hairnet." Nici

cursed again before going into the restroom and slamming the door.

"Community service," TJ whispered. "I wonder what she did."

"You three come here to chat or to work?" Edna barked from across the room.

"Work," Annabelle said quickly and hurried forward to be handed a hairnet and a soup ladle.

"We're about to open," the supervisor said. "You," she said pointing at TJ. "You're in charge of buns and you," she said pointing at Chloe, "you'll be helping run dishes. When we run out of soup, we all help clean up this place. Is that understood?"

"Perfectly," Chloe and TJ said in unison as Nici came out of the bathroom.

"And you," Edna said. "You're going straight to the dish room and start cleaning. And," she said as Nici started to complain, "if you say one word, I'm calling the sheriff."

"Jail looks good right now," the young woman said under her breath as she walked past Chloe and then did a double take. Edna had gone to open the doors. "What are you doing here?" Nici demanded of Chloe.

"We always helped at the soup kitchen with our grandmother."

"No, what are you doing in Whitehorse?"

"Spending time with my sisters over the holidays." Chloe wondered why she was answering Nici's rude questions. It was just such a surprise seeing her here.

"So you aren't staying," Nici said.

"Nicole Kent, you've got two seconds to get into the dish room," Edna called and Nici scooted off after an eye roll and a curse.

"Charming," TJ said as she pulled on her hairnet and the plastic gloves she would be wearing while handing out buns.

"I never understood what Justin saw in her," Annabelle said.

Chloe watched her go into the dish room. "They were a lot alike. Both on the outside looking in."

"Alike? Nici from one of the poorest families and Justin from one of the wealthiest? He comes from one of the largest ranches around here," Annabelle said. "His family was rich compared to most and his father still is."

"I doubt Bert Calhoun would feel that way," TJ said. "He lost his wife at a young age and apparently now he's lost both sons."

"You know what I mean," Annabelle said. "Wealth-wise."

"But Justin always felt as if he didn't matter," Chloe said. "I would imagine Nici felt the same way."

Edna began barking orders so they went to work, but Chloe couldn't help thinking about Justin and what she'd learned had happened to him and his family after she'd left. She knew that he and his older brother hadn't gotten along, but she refused to believe Justin had anything to do with Drew's death.

IT DIDN'T TAKE Justin long to pack. Quitting his job hadn't been that hard either. Saddle tramps like him were a dime a dozen. The rancher would be able to pick up help easily before calving season when he really would need it.

After throwing everything into his pickup, he slid behind the wheel wondering why he hadn't done this sooner. The reason was staring him in the face. He hadn't wanted to know the truth about his brother's death. It had been easier to run away.

He sighed as he started the truck and pointed it west. *Why now?* It was the question that had been nagging at him all morning. *Tell me this isn't about some kiss that was so long ago it was like another world.*

Justin laughed to himself as he left the dirt road and hit the two-lane blacktop. Hearing Chloe's voice had brought it all back. Those few weeks of happiness before his life had gone to hell in a handbasket. Maybe he was trying to relive those moments—as crazy as it sounded. He was too much of a realist to think he could.

But he'd been hiding out from the past for too long. He was going home—to all that entailed. Just the thought of seeing his father set his teeth on edge. But he was no longer afraid of the past. It was the truth that woke him in a cold sweat in the middle of the night. What *had* happened the day his brother was killed?

"GRANDMOTHER WOULD BE so proud," Annabelle said as they tossed their hairnets in the trash, pulled on their coats and left the now-clean soup kitchen.

"You're being awfully quiet," TJ said as Chloe climbed into the back seat of Annabelle's SUV and TJ took shotgun. She turned in her seat to look back at her. "Are you angry with me for calling Justin?"

"No. It was nice talking to him. But that ship sailed a long time ago."

"Don't say that," Annabelle cut in as she slid behind the wheel and started the motor. "Look at me and Dawson. I left him even when he worked so hard to buy me an engagement ring and roses to ask me to marry him. I thought he'd never forgive me. He said I broke his heart." Her voice cracked with emotion and tears flooded her blue eyes. "But we found our way back to each other."

"I wonder why Justin didn't marry Nici," Chloe said.

"Who knows if they were even really engaged," Annabelle said and scoffed. "That's just what Nici said after they broke up. As far as I know that's as close as she's gotten to marriage."

"Maybe she spends too much time in jail," TJ joked.

"You two have certainly gotten caught up on local gossip," Chloe said. Thinking of Nici made her uncomfortable. The woman was her own worst enemy. But weren't they all that way sometimes?

"So are you going to tell us what is going on

with you?" TJ asked as she buckled her seat belt and looked at Chloe in her side mirror.

"Why?" Annabelle said. "What's going on with Chloe?" She shot a questioning look in the rearview mirror at her oldest sister.

"I lost my job," Chloe said, glad to have the secret out.

"What do you mean you 'lost it'?" TJ said.

"I was laid off with a bunch of others." She looked out the window as Annabelle drove through the small western town of Whitehorse. It wasn't that long ago that she was here for her grandmother's funeral. Before that, she'd seldom returned except for quick visits. Like her sisters she'd wanted to conquer the world—far from Whitehorse, Montana.

Annabelle had become a supermodel with her face on the covers of magazines—until recently giving it up to be with her old high school boyfriend, rancher Dawson Rogers. The two were perfect for each other. Chloe wondered why it had taken her sister so long to realize it.

As for TJ, she'd become a *New York Times* bestselling author who also only recently left the big city life after falling in love. She now lived in a tiny cabin in the woods until she and her fiancé could get a larger place built up in the Little Rockies.

Chloe had become an investigative journalist and had worked her way up through bigger papers until she'd found herself working for one of the largest in Southern California. But with the way print newspapers were going recently, she'd been laid off with a dozen others and the thought of looking for another newspaper job… She said as much to her sisters.

"I'm so sorry," Annabelle said. "What are you going to do?"

Chloe let out a bark of a laugh. "I have no idea. I have enough money saved that I don't have to worry about it for a while."

"You can stay in grandmother's house as long as you want," Annabelle said.

Grandmother's house. She had to smile at that. Their grandmother Frannie had left the house to only Annabelle, which had caused friction between them but ultimately brought them together.

"It's funny how things work out," she said as her sister pulled up in front of the house in question. Annabelle, with help from friends, had refurbished the house. It did have a feeling of home, Chloe had to admit, since the three of them were raised in this house. It was a large two-story with four bedrooms, two up and two down. It sat among large old cottonwoods and backed to the Milk River in an area affectionately called "Millionaire's Row."

Not that any houses in Whitehorse were even close to a million. The homes were conservative like the rural people who lived in the area. And right now, Chloe had to admit, the town looked almost charming with its mantle of fresh snow and holiday lights.

"Would you mind if I borrowed your SUV?" Chloe

asked as her sister pulled up into the driveway of their grandmother's house. "There's somewhere I need to go."

JUSTIN DROVE ACROSS eastern Montana trying to imagine the rolling prairie landscape when thousands of buffalo roamed the area. Unfortunately, they'd all been killed off. He'd seen photos of their bones stacked in huge piles next to the railroad at Whitehorse.

His great-great-grandfather had been on one of the original cattle drives that brought longhorns to the area from Texas. He'd heard about how lush the grass was back then. His father's family had settled the land, giving birth to the Calhoun Cattle Company. He still got a lump in this throat when he thought about his legacy.

It hadn't been easy to give it up and simply walk away. Kind of like ripping out his heart. He loved the land, the ranch history, the feeling of being a part of something bigger than himself. He'd always felt more of a kinship with the ranch than his brother had—not that their father noticed.

So he'd left, since his heart had already been decimated over his brother's death—and his father's accusations. Now all that grief and regret had settled in his chest like a weight he couldn't throw off. Five years had done little to lessen the pain. But he had grown up in that time. He was his own man now, something he could have never been with his older

brother constantly reminding him that he was the
little brother, the one his father didn't put his faith
or his love into.

By early afternoon he looked up to see Whitehorse, the tall grain bins next to the railroad silhou-
etted against the winter sky. He slowed his pickup,
wanting to take it all in. Memories, both good and bad,
assailed him. Home.

He took a deep breath, telling himself he was
going to settle things once and for all, starting with
the people he'd hurt.

THE *MILK RIVER COURIER*, the town's only newspaper,
was lodged in a small brick building along the main
road. Chloe felt a rush of excitement as she pushed
open the door. Being an investigative reporter was
in her blood. She loved digging for information and
couldn't wait to get into the newspaper's archives.

The smell of ink and paper filled her nostrils, the
sound of clicking keyboards like music to her ears.
It was early in the week so the small staff was busy
trying to put together the weekly edition. She was
led to the archives where she settled in, determined
to find out what she could.

Chloe reread the first story about Andrew "Drew"
Calhoun's death. It was short and clearly had little
more information in it than what she'd found on the
sheriff's blog that had also run in the paper.

Drew was found dead at 11:22 p.m. on that Saturday night. He'd been shot. It was unclear by whom.

He was pronounced dead by the coroner at the scene. The investigation was continuing.

She read through what few stories followed, realizing that no one from the paper had gotten anywhere if they'd even tried to investigate the death. This was a small town and Bert Calhoun was a wealthy rancher. The paper had let the story die. It didn't take long to realize little information had become public. The small weekly printed what was called the cop reports, but didn't dig any deeper so skimmed only the surface of the news.

Chloe didn't blame the staff. She understood, because even with larger newspapers there were some situations that were touchy. She'd always had trouble treading lightly. Like now. She wanted answers and she realized there was only one place to go. She couldn't bear the idea that Justin had been blamed for his brother's death—even if he'd never been arrested for it. She had to know the truth. It was inherent in her DNA. And this was Justin. The cowboy she'd shared that one amazing winter kiss with all those years ago. A girl didn't forget things like that.

JUSTIN FOUND THE Kent house without any trouble. It was a large old three-story wooden structure that needed paint and the porch fixed. It looked exactly as he remembered it.

He had no idea if Nicole even still lived in Whitehorse. He'd made a point of not keeping in touch with anyone from home. As he walked up the unshoveled, snow-packed walk to the door, he saw a faded curtain twitch. The door was opened before he even reached it.

"I guess it's a day for surprises," Nici said as she leaned against the doorjamb. "What are you doing back here?"

"It's good to see you too, Nici." She hadn't changed from her dyed black hair to her belligerent attitude. He had to smile. "Buy you a coffee?"

"Make it a beer and you're on."

The last place he wanted to go was a bar where he might be recognized. He pulled into the local convenience store, ran in and came back out with a six-pack.

"Maybe you haven't heard, but Montana has an open container law," she said as he handed her the beer.

"Then you'd better not open one until we reach the lake," he said and started the truck.

She immediately opened a beer, just as he knew she would. They said little on the drive out to Nelson Reservoir. He and Nici used to come out here all the time at night in the summer. He would be tired from working the ranch all day under his father's unrelenting supervision. He'd need to unwind and Nici was always up for it.

"Remember swimming naked out here late at night?" Nici asked as he parked at the edge of the boat ramp and turned off the engine. She was holding the beer can, looking out at the frozen expanse of cold white.

"Doesn't look too appealing at the moment," he commented and she handed him a beer. He settled back in the seat, opened the can and took a drink. It almost felt like old times.

"What are you doing here?" Nici asked, sounding worried about him.

He turned to look at her and smiled. "I've come home to face the music."

"You didn't kill Drew."

Justin said nothing as he took another drink and turned his attention again to a more pleasant memory from the past. "Remember that one night we got caught out here by that camper?"

Nici chuckled. "Apparently the man had never been young. Either that or he didn't like his teenage sons ogling me as I came out of the water bareassed naked."

He laughed. "You always liked shocking people."

"Still do." She glanced over at him. "Did you think I might have changed?"

Justin turned a little in his seat. His gaze softened as he looked at her. "I'm sorry if I hurt you."

Nici huffed. "You join AA or something? If this is about making amends—"

"I'm serious. I know you hoped that things were more serious between us…"

She took a long drink of her beer without looking at him.

"You were my best friend. Hell, my only female friend."

"But not good enough to marry." When she turned to look at him there were tears in her dark eyes. She made an angry swipe at them, finished her beer and pulled another can free of the plastic holder.

"I loved you. I still do."

Nici stopped and looked over at him.

"I still think of you as my best girl friend." He smiled. "I've often wondered what kind of trouble you've been into back here in Montana. I've missed you."

She stared at him. "You make it hard to hate you."

"Good." He touched her shoulder. "I feel like I left you high and dry. I didn't mean to do that."

"You married Margie." She made it sound like an accusation.

"I know. A mistake. I ended up hurting her too." He shook his head. "I did a lot of things I'm not proud of. That's why I'm back."

"To make amends."

"To straighten out a few things," he said. "I can't undo anything I've done. All I can do is say I'm sorry. So how *have* you been?"

She laughed. "Not great. I spent the morning doing community service. Don't ask." He saw that it was hard for her to admit it. "I should have gone to college or gotten a job. I should have left Whitehorse."

"It's not too late."

"Isn't it?"

"No. So what's keeping you here?" he asked. "A man?"

Nici shook her head. "Inertia. I guess I just needed someone to give me a swift kick to get me moving."

"Consider this your kick." They drank their beer for a moment, both lost in their own thoughts. "There's something I need to ask you," he finally said.

"About me and Drew." She shook her head and looked way. "I knew that was coming." Her dark eyes filled with hurt and anger. "I didn't shoot him."

"But you were at the ranch that night."

She didn't deny it. "Drew was a bastard, but I suspect you already know that."

"What happened that night?"

Nici sighed and looked away. "Why are you just now asking me this?"

"Because I have to know. I should have asked five years ago."

"What do you think happened?" she snapped. "I knew why Drew called me. It was nothing more than a booty call." She turned to stare him down. "I knew he was just doing it to hurt you, but I didn't care. You were breaking my heart. You think I didn't know that you were never going to marry me?"

Justin felt as if she'd thrust a knife into his chest. "I'm sorry. You meant so much to me—"

"Just not enough." She licked her lips, her throat

working for a moment. "That's the story of my life. I've never felt like enough."

"I know that feeling."

She continued as if she hadn't heard him. "I've let men use me…" Her voice broke.

The pickup cab filled with a heavy silence. Outside the wind picked up and began to lift the new snow into the air.

"I hate that you feel I was one of those men."

She looked over at him, her gaze softening. "I wanted more so I was angry, but I never felt that way about…us."

He finally asked, "So you met him that night out at the ranch."

She nodded solemnly. "It was just as I thought. He got what he wanted and told me to leave."

Justin had been in the horse barn when he'd heard the shots and looked out. He'd seen her drive away. He'd run to his brother's cabin some distance from the main house and found him. Only minutes later his father burst in to find him holding the gun. He'd always wondered if Bert Calhoun had seen Nici driving away and never said anything.

Justin had kept his mouth shut as well, covering for her. He'd never told anyone—not even the sheriff. "Did you see anyone else? Or did Drew mention anything that might have been going on with him?" For a moment, he thought she wasn't going to answer.

"Before I left, he got a call. He stepped outside

the cabin to take it. He seemed upset and even more in a hurry for me to leave."

"You don't know who it was from?" Justin asked.

Nici shook her head. "It was a woman—I know that. Drew didn't say much on the phone, but the way he said it… Why did you never tell anyone about seeing me that night?"

He shrugged. "You'd already been in trouble with the law. I was afraid…" He didn't finish the sentence.

Nici reached over and touched his arm. "I didn't shoot him. I would have gone to the sheriff if I'd known that everyone would think you did."

"It wouldn't have done any good," he said. "Even you can't be sure I didn't kill him."

She studied him for a long moment. "If I'd been you, I would have killed him. Only I wouldn't have stopped firing until the gun was empty. He deserved so much worse."

Chapter Three

Justin drove out to the Rogers Ranch. Dawson was a couple years younger. They'd grown up just down the road from each other. Of all the people he'd known, Justin trusted Dawson the most since they'd been friends since they were kids.

As he drove up into his old friend's yard, Dawson came out of the barn wiping his hands on a rag. Past him, Justin could see an old tractor with some of its parts lying on a bench nearby.

"You still trying to get that thing running?" he said as he got out of his truck and approached the rancher.

Dawson wiped his right hand on his canvas pants and extended it. They shook hands both smiling at each other. "I swear that tractor is going to be the end of me," he said, glancing toward the barn. "I know I should get rid of it but we're like old friends." His gaze came back to Justin. "Speaking of old friends…"

Justin took a breath and let it out before he said. "I needed to come back and take care of a few things."

Dawson nodded. "You need a place to stay?"

"I'd appreciate it. I could stay at the hotel in town but—"

"No reason to. You know you're welcome here. I have a guest room in the house."

"I'd prefer the bunkhouse if you don't mind."

Dawson seemed to study him for a moment. "I was just headed up to the main house. If my mother heard you were staying here and she didn't get to see you, she'd skin me alive."

Justin laughed and shook his head. "Worse, she'd skin *me* alive."

"Why don't we hop into my pickup?" his friend suggested. "I want to hear all about where you've been and what you've been doing."

"Wish it was worth telling. Let's just say I've been on the run, but I'm back."

"To stay?" Dawson asked.

"Hard to say."

Dawson slapped him on the shoulder as they neared his truck. "Well, I hope you're home for good. How long have you been in town?"

"Just got in earlier."

"Well, then you haven't heard. Annabelle Clementine and I are engaged."

"No kidding," Justin said. "Congratulations. I'm glad to hear that. I always thought you and Annabelle belonged together. I heard her sister Chloe's here for the holidays."

SHERIFF MCCALL CRAWFORD motioned Chloe into her office. "You look so serious, maybe you'd better close the door."

She smiled as she closed the door and took the chair the sheriff offered her. "I'm here about the Drew Calhoun shooting."

McCall nodded. "What about it?"

"I'd like to see the file." The sheriff raised a brow. "It happened five years ago and was ruled an accident. I wouldn't think you'd have a problem with my seeing it."

"I have to ask why you're interested," McCall said. "As a reporter?"

"I'm currently not a reporter for a newspaper," she said, but feeling like whatever had pushed her into that career would always be with her. Curiosity. The kind that killed cats. "I'm taking some time off to consider my options."

"What exactly are you looking for then with Drew Calhoun's death?" the sheriff asked.

"Answers."

McCall said nothing for a few moments. "Is there anyone who might want to get you involved in his death?"

She thought of Justin. "Not that I know of."

"So why get involved?"

"It's what I do. I'm an investigative reporter. Maybe it is the years of doing this for a living, but I feel there might be more to the story."

"There isn't. I investigated Drew Calhoun's death. It was an accident."

Chloe studied her for a moment. She'd heard good things about McCall. "Then there shouldn't be a problem with looking into the case."

"I would be happy to tell you anything you'd like to know." McCall leaned back in her chair. "Ask away."

"I understand Bert Calhoun believes his son Justin fired the fatal shot. Was there gunshot residue on Justin's hands and clothing?"

"Some."

Chloe blinked. She hadn't been expecting that.

The sheriff continued. "Why don't I tell you exactly what's in the report? Drew was found by his brother, Justin, in a cabin on the property. The gun belonged to Drew. Justin said he heard two gunshots and went to investigate."

"*Two* shots?"

"One bullet caught Drew in the heart, the other lodged in the wall by the door, which he was facing. Both were from the same gun, the one Justin said he found his brother holding in his lap."

"So how did Justin—"

"Drew was still alive, according to his brother, and trying to fire the gun a third time. Justin rushed to him and took the gun away from him and called for help. But before the ambulance and EMTs could get there, Drew died."

Chloe sat back. "So why did I hear Bert Calhoun thinks Justin killed his brother?"

The sheriff shook her head. "I've found grieving parents especially have trouble accepting their child's death. They don't want to face it. They tell me that their son knew guns, had since he was a boy. That he wouldn't have been stupid enough to shoot himself." She shrugged. "The truth is accidents happen all the time. People get careless."

"Was there any sign of a struggle?" Chloe asked.

McCall glanced away and Chloe knew she'd hit on something. "Apparently Drew had a run-in with someone earlier that night. He'd been drinking, according to the blood alcohol level hours later. He had a split lip, a cut over one eye. The eye was nearly swollen shut, which could also explain why he was careless with the gun. He had lacerations on his arms and jaw."

"Lacerations?"

The sheriff met her gaze. "Scratches."

"Like from fingernails?"

"The coroner said that was definitely an option," she said noncommittally.

"Do you have any idea who he tangled with that night?" Chloe asked.

She shook her head. "But he and his brother had been heard arguing earlier in the day. When Justin was questioned his knuckles were skinned and he had a bruise on his forehead. He admitted to having argued with his brother but swears he didn't beat him up. As for his own injuries, he said they were self-inflicted. He alleged that he'd taken out his temper on a tree out by the pond on the ranch property. When tests were run on his hands, fragments of tree resin were found."

"So he was telling the truth," she said. "Did you pass all of this on to his father?"

"I did. But like I said—"

"Bert had his mind made up." She nodded. "Isn't it possible that someone fired the shot that would kill Drew, dropped the gun and ran? Drew picked up the gun and fired the shot that was found embedded in the wall by the door?"

"Possible. Justin said he heard the sound of a vehicle engine as he was calling 911. But we found no evidence another person had been in that room let alone shot Drew."

"You ruled it an accident." She met the sheriff's gaze. "It sounds more like a suicide."

The sheriff bristled. "That's not what the evidence led me to. I wasn't alone. The coroner agreed."

"But you also don't want this to be a suicide."

McCall sighed. "No one wants to tell a father that his son killed himself, that's true. But there was no suicide note. No apparent depression or talk of suicide. People who knew him didn't believe Drew would have purposely taken his own life. Also there is no evidence that Drew was trying to kill himself," McCall said. "Alcohol was involved. His wouldn't be the first accident with a firearm when the user has been drinking."

Chloe sat forward. "But what if he was trying to defend himself?"

"From whom?"

"That's what I don't know, but the shot in the direction of the door bothers me." She could see that it had bothered the sheriff, as well.

"I believe he was impaired enough that he didn't have control over the gun," McCall said.

Drew had been in a fight and he was drunk. She supposed he could have gotten his gun out, thinking whoever had given him the beating might want to finish him off. And in his drunken state shot the wall and then himself as he fumbled with the gun.

"Did you know Drew Calhoun?" the sheriff asked.

She shook her head. "He was older so he was out of high school before I got there. I've heard stories about him. I know he and Justin didn't get along."

The sheriff nodded. "I'm not sure what you plan to do with this information, but I hope you're sensitive to the pain a tragedy like this leaves in a community, not to mention how a father is still struggling to deal with his loss."

Chloe had conflicting emotions when it came to the case. What she knew of Drew assured her that he had no reason to want to kill himself. He had been arrogant, wild and his father's favorite. He'd been spoiled all his life. Suicide didn't seem likely. Not that people who have shown no sign of suicidal tendencies previously don't take their lives in weak moments.

"I lived with a lot of what-ifs in my life, not knowing the truth about my own father," McCall said.

"But then you found out the truth."

The sheriff nodded. "Which led to other truths perhaps I hadn't wanted to know. I found out that whenever you go digging into something like this, it can be dangerous, especially if you go into it believing one thing only to find out you're wrong. But I can see that your mind is made up." She got to her feet. "Let me get you the information."

As Chloe was leaving the sheriff's office, she almost collided with a man in uniform. He caught her as she stumbled against him. As her gaze rose to his face, she felt a shock. "Kelly?"

"That's Deputy Locke to you," he said seriously. "Don't look so surprised."

Shocked was more like it. It felt like running headlong into the solid brick wall of her past. All the pain the man had caused her. She'd hated Kelly Locke. For a moment, she couldn't speak. She'd thought he'd left town and said as much.

"I came back. Seems you did the same thing."

She stared at him, her throat constricting. Everyone had people in their past who'd helped shape them. If anything, Kelly Locke had made her the cynical woman she'd become. It was what made her dig for stories, looking for the truth. The truth meant more to her than anything. She'd already lived with the lies because of him.

"You like the uniform?" he asked, making her realize she'd been staring.

"I never thought of you like this," she stammered.

"You thought of me?" He grinned and brushed back a lock of blond hair from his blue eyes. When she didn't respond, he said, "So what are you doing here?"

She opened her mouth, closed it. "Just stopped in to see the sheriff."

"Anything I can help you with?"

"No." She said it a little too quickly.

He raised a brow. "If you don't want to tell me…"

The shock was starting to wear off. "I'm sure you're busy with keeping Whitehorse safe from jaywalkers."

"Funny," he said as he puffed up, his hand going to the weapon on his hip. "But then again, you always did like the one-liners."

She looked into his handsome face and thought as she had years ago how unfair it was that Kelly Locke could look so good and yet be such a jackass. But it was worse than that. She knew how cruel the man could be since she'd stupidly dated him at one point. That he was now a deputy and armed made her a little uneasy—especially given the way things had ended between them.

"So how long have you been a deputy?"

He grinned. "Almost six years."

"That long." It would mean that he'd been a deputy when Drew Calhoun was killed.

"I'm the strong arm of the law," he said, his gaze meeting hers and holding it. "Which means you'd best watch yourself." He lowered his voice and leaned closer so the dispatcher couldn't hear. She caught a cloying waft of men's cologne. "I'd hate to have to cuff you and take you for a ride in the back of my patrol car."

"I'll keep that in mind." With that, she stepped past him and headed for the exit. She could feel herself trembling, remembering what he'd done to her. She didn't have to look back to know he was watching her. His gaze burned into her back. The man gave her more than the creeps. He scared her.

Chapter Four

When Chloe returned to their grandmother's house, she found Annabelle in the kitchen baking cookies and TJ editing a manuscript at the table.

"Why didn't you tell me that Kelly Locke is a cop?" Chloe demanded when she walked in and saw her two sisters.

They looked up in surprise. "He isn't a cop—he's a sheriff's deputy," Annabelle said.

"Same thing! He carries a gun and a badge!" she cried.

"I take it that the uniform doesn't make your old boyfriend look even better to you? Has he changed?" TJ asked. Not enough, Chloe thought. But then again she'd never told her sisters the extent of Kelly's malice after they'd broken up.

"It's his personality that's the problem." She shuddered.

"He was always so angry, so close to the edge that I was on pins and needles all the time you were dating," TJ said. "He'd go off for no reason. He was always looking for a fight. If anyone looked at him cross-eyed—"

"Wow, he really did set you both off," Annabelle said. "I always thought he was really cute and built too. What did he do this time? Arrest you for throwing snowballs at cars like some of us used to do?"

"You don't know how unfunny that is. I ran into him at the sheriff's office," she said. "He threatened to handcuff me and get me into the back of his patrol car."

"What were you doing at the sheriff's office unless he did arrest you?" Annabelle asked.

Chloe saw that both sisters were studying her.

"What's going on?" TJ asked suspiciously.

She tried to wave it off, but could see neither sister was going to let her get away with it. "I'm looking into Drew Calhoun's death."

"Why would you do that?" TJ and Annabelle asked in unison.

"That is so annoying when you two do that," she said.

"Is this about Justin?" Annabelle asked.

"I'm just curious about Drew's case," she said as she opened the refrigerator, pulled out the orange juice and poured herself a glass. She wasn't thirsty. She just needed something to do with her hands. It was hard to stall without keeping her hands busy.

"Just curious?" TJ said. "Are you looking for a job?"

Taking a drink, she turned slowly to meet her sister's gaze. "I'm not sure what I want to do next."

"Chloe? You aren't thinking of quitting print journalism, are you?"

"Maybe you haven't heard but newspapers are struggling right now," Chloe began and was quickly interrupted.

"With your track record?" TJ asked in surprise. "You can get a job almost anywhere, maybe a smaller paper but—"

"I'm not sure what I want to do," she said. "Maybe I just need a break."

Annabelle laughed. "You're falling in love with Whitehorse all over again, aren't you? You don't want to leave."

Chloe rolled her eyes. "I wouldn't go that far, but I am enjoying being here with the two of you." She went over to where Annabelle was taking cookies hot from the oven off the pan and setting them out to cool. She had to smile. Her younger sister had never shown any interest in cooking or baking growing up.

When they were kids, TJ had taken up cooking because their grandmother was no cook. Chloe had been the baker. There was something so satisfying about whipping up a batch of cookies. Plus you got to eat them while they were still warm. She'd forgotten how much she'd enjoyed it since she seldom baked for herself.

"Sugar cookies for Dawson," Annabelle said proudly.

"And for your big sister Chloe," she said, taking a cookie. "You're getting good at this. These are delicious."

Her sister lit up at the praise. "I figure I'll branch out into cooking. Willie has promised to teach me a few of Dawson's favorite dishes."

"You couldn't ask for a better teacher," Chloe said of Dawson's mother.

TJ was studying her again. "I know you, Chloe. Unless you have a project, you will go crazy between now and the wedding. We don't want that."

She realized that her sister was giving her permission to dig into the Drew Calhoun case. Like she needed her permission, she thought, but wasn't about to voice it. Annabelle and TJ would be busy and out of her hair. She was her own woman. She could do whatever she wanted.

"But are you sure there isn't more to this quest you're on?" TJ asked, studying her closely. "Like Justin?"

Chloe had to smile. Her sister knew her so well. "I might as well hang around for a while. Anyway, we have a wedding coming up, right?"

"That's what we wanted to tell you," Annabelle said excitedly. "We have a surprise."

Chloe had already told them that she didn't like surprises. Often it meant change. Like when their parents had been killed and they'd been shipped to Whitehorse to live with a grandmother they didn't even know existed before then. Grandma Frannie had been wonderful, but she'd definitely been a surprise.

What was she thinking? Frannie had continued to be a surprise.

"We're going to have a double wedding!" Annabelle announced, smiling broadly, her eyes glittering as she reached over and grasped TJ's hand.

"Congratulations!" Chloe said, glad for the change of subject. "This is wonderful. What can I do to help?"

The conversation quickly shifted to the double wedding: who, what, where, when.

"We need to find you a dress to wear," Annabelle was saying.

"I thought you both wanted small weddings?" she asked.

"It can be small but elegant," Annabelle said.

Chloe looked at TJ. "You and Silas are good with this?"

Her sister laughed. "My mountain man does own a tux, you know."

She looked at them and felt her heart swell. "I am so happy for both of you."

"So what have you found out so far?" TJ asked as Chloe joined her at the table.

"I just did a little research on Drew Calhoun's death," she said. "There wasn't much in the local paper so I talked to the sheriff. It was interesting—and disturbing."

"In what way?" Annabelle asked as she brought over a plate of cookies and joined them.

"No real answers. I can understand why McCall ruled it an accident, but it definitely left me wondering. I'm sure that's the problem Justin's dad is having with it, as well. Did you know that someone beat up Drew that night before he was shot? He had cuts and bruises, a black eye and scratches on his face and arms that the coroner said appeared to be from fingernails."

"So some woman beat him up?" Annabelle said.

"I'd say he definitely tangled with someone or maybe a mountain lion," she said. "I'd love to know who was responsible. But it makes me think that it's why Drew, who was drunk, was in the cabin with his gun."

"Maybe he was going after whoever beat him up," TJ suggested.

"Or thought they were coming after him," Annabelle added.

Chloe sighed. "We might never know. He wasn't dead though when Justin found him. According to Justin, he took the gun away from him—that's how his fingerprints ended up on the gun. It also explained trace amounts of gunpowder residue on Justin's hands."

"I heard that one of the reasons Bert thinks Justin shot his brother was because he found him standing over Drew holding the gun," Annabelle said.

"That would do it," TJ agreed.

"Also Justin and Drew had a fight earlier in the day," Chloe said.

"What convinced the sheriff that Justin didn't do it?" TJ, the mystery/thriller writer, asked.

"Before I left her office, McCall gave me a copy

of the coroner's report. I've only glanced at it, but Drew was shot at close range in the chest. There was another shot fired either before or after. This one in the opposite direction. The bullet lodged in the wall next to the door."

"That's odd," TJ said.

"That's what I thought. I suggested to the sheriff that someone shot Drew with his gun, then dropped it in his lap to make it look like a suicide and was leaving, not realizing Drew was still alive. He picked up the gun and fired at his would-be killer. His shot went wild. He was still holding the gun when Justin appeared minutes later and took it away from him. Justin said he heard a vehicle motor leaving after he found Drew, but apparently no one else did since his father found him not long after, holding the gun."

"Or Drew was drunk and angry. He fired the shot at the door before turning the gun on himself," TJ said and shrugged. "Like you said, we'll probably never know."

"But what if someone got away with murder?" Chloe said.

Neither sister said anything for a moment.

"Wait, if you really think Drew was murdered, won't this be dangerous?" Annabelle said.

"Maybe even more dangerous if Justin Calhoun decides to come to the New Year's Eve Masquerade Dance," TJ said. "There are apparently plenty of people in this town who believe he killed his brother.

Justin might be the last person who wants you playing investigative reporter into his brother's death."

"WE'VE GOT TROUBLE."

"I heard. Justin Calhoun is back in town. Someone saw him buying beer at the convenience store. Nici Kent was with him."

"Bigger trouble than that."

"Chloe Clementine. She's an investigative reporter from some big California newspaper. She spent time at the local newspaper wanting to know about Drew Calhoun's death. Then she went over to the sheriff's office. I heard the sheriff gave her the coroner's report on his death."

"So what? The sheriff ruled it an accident. It's been five years. It isn't as if they would reopen the case because of some nosey reporter. Just keep your cool. Nothing's going to come of this."

"But what if this Clementine gets too close to the truth?"

"Then I'll take care of her. You worry too much. Drew Calhoun got what was coming to him. There is no reason anyone would suspect we were involved. So chill out. She's going to be asking a lot of questions, but we don't know anything, right?"

"Right. It's just that after five years—"

"I'm telling you it's nothing. It's over. We're all in the clear." But even as he mouthed the words, he could tell that they weren't in the clear. There was a weak link and he was going to have to take care of it.

After disconnecting he considered his options. He wouldn't do anything until he was forced to. Maybe all this would blow over. Or not. Still there was cause for concern. Something must have brought Justin Calhoun back to Whitehorse. The timing bothered him. He returns and this investigative reporter gets interested? There had to be a connection. Or someone had talked.

Chapter Five

The next morning, Chloe woke more determined than ever. She knew her sisters were right about the possible danger, but that wasn't going to stop her. In the first place, she didn't believe that Justin was guilty no matter what anyone thought. In the second place, she couldn't shake the feeling that something was wrong with the accidental death ruling.

Yesterday, she'd gotten the impression that the sheriff had thought it was a suicide but was willing to let the coroner rule it accidental. Bert didn't believe that any more than he would have believed that his oldest son shot himself.

If she was right, someone had murdered Drew and gotten away with it. All she had to do was find out who wanted him dead five years ago. Even as she thought it, she recalled what the sheriff had said about Justin and Drew having an argument earlier in the day.

What if she was wrong about Justin and her investigation ended up leading her straight to him? Wasn't that what the sheriff had been trying to warn her about?

It was a chance she was going to have to take.

She'd stayed up late last night going over the case file and coroner's report on Drew Calhoun's death. So when the phone rang, it took her a moment to wake up, let alone find it and answer.

As she hit Accept, she realized it could be Justin. "Hello?"

Silence.

"Hello?" She blinked at the clock beside her bed. Two thirty in the morning? A wrong number? A drunk butt-dial after the bars closed?

She started to hang up when she heard a raspy whisper and couldn't tell if it was a man or a woman on the line. "Stop nosing into things that aren't your business. Drew Calhoun is dead. Leave it alone or you'll regret it."

"Who is this?" she demanded. But the caller was gone. She felt a chill as she disconnected. She hadn't expected word to get out so soon that she was looking into Drew's death—let alone to get a threatening phone call. Why would someone be worried about what she might find unless Drew really was murdered?

With a shudder she realized she just might have heard from the killer who would be watching her and waiting for her to get too close.

IT TOOK A while for her to get back to sleep. With daylight though, she was even more determined to get to the truth.

But where to begin? A name came to mind. She groaned, dreading it, but if anyone knew something back then, it just might be the woman Justin was seeing five years ago. She showered, dressed and had a quick breakfast before her sisters got up. It didn't take but one phone call to find out where Nici Kent was now living. It was a short walk, since crossing the entire town took only about fifteen minutes on foot.

Nici answered the door with a scowl. "Really?" She didn't look any different than she had yesterday at the soup kitchen—except she wasn't wearing a hairnet.

"Really," Chloe said. "I need to talk to you."

"I can't imagine why."

Chloe smiled. "Let me in and maybe you'll find out."

Nici shook her head. "My sister's kid's been squalling all morning at the top of his lungs. You want to talk? Then we'd better take a walk." She grabbed her coat and, pulling it on, closed the door and started down the steps.

They walked toward the park near the river.

"I was hoping you might be able to help me," Chloe said. The morning was cold and clear. She could see her breath with each word. Hands stuffed into her coat pockets, she debated how to get Nici to talk.

"Help you?" The woman gave her a skeptical look. "I doubt you'd be dumb enough to ask me for money, so you must need—"

"Information."

Nici laughed. "What kind of information is it you think I can give you?"

They'd reached the park and were almost to the footbridge that crossed the river. Everything close to the water was covered with a thick coating of frost, making the world around them a winter white. "Drew Calhoun."

The woman stopped walking to turn to look at her. "Why would you be asking about him?"

Chloe could see that she was going to have to lay all her cards on the table. "I got a call in the middle of last night from someone warning me to stop investigating Drew Calhoun's death. You wouldn't know anything about that call, would you?"

Nici said nothing as she climbed up on the bridge.

Chloe followed, stepping up onto the snow-covered bridge and starting across the frozen river. "You were dating his brother, Justin, five years ago. If anyone knows what was going on with Drew and his brother it would be you."

Nici stopped so abruptly, Chloe almost collided with her. It took her a moment to get her balance on the slippery snow.

"What is it you're after?" Nici demanded.

"The truth."

The woman scoffed and began walking again, stopping in the middle of the bridge to look down. "It's over. Best leave it alone."

"That's what the caller said, but is it over? Is it over for Justin?"

Leaning on the metal railing, Nici looked at her, her eyes narrowing. "I know about you and Justin."

"There isn't much to know," Chloe said. "But I'd like to see him vindicated."

"So it's like that," the woman said, studying her. "You know he's back in town." She chuckled when she saw Chloe's surprised expression. "So you didn't know. He said he's come back to make amends. That tell you anything?"

"I don't believe he killed his brother."

Nici shrugged. "You could be right. But you also could be wrong. Drew was one mean bastard to Justin from the time they were kids."

"Justin can't be the only person who had reason to hate Drew. What about you?"

"Me?" Nici shook her head and laughed.

"Drew had scratches on him that the coroner believed were from a woman's fingernails."

Nici looked down at her gloved hands. When she looked up she smiled. "Sounds like he got what he deserved."

"Let's assume you didn't kill him, then how about one of his friends or associates?" Chloe asked wriggling her toes in her boots to keep her feet warm. Nici didn't seem to be the least bit cold even though she was wearing a much less insulated coat and thinner gloves.

"Friends? I'm not sure Drew had any. But associates…"

"Yes?"

Nici met her gaze. "You do realize that there are some people in town who won't like what you're doing."

"I'm not worried about them."

"Maybe you should be."

"Tell me about his associates," Chloe said.

Nici took her sweet time, but finally said, "There were a group of guys he played poker with. I heard he got caught cheating." She shrugged. "The man who caught him was one who'd lost the most money to Drew, a man named Monte Decker. He works at the bank."

Chloe didn't know him. "Anyone else?" She waited, cold, her cheeks and nose feeling icy and her skin stinging. The air along the frozen creek felt as if it was at least ten degrees colder than in town.

"Al Duncan. He bought a horse from Drew and later found out that it was lame. The day he bought it, the horse was so full of drugs, he couldn't tell. Drew refused to give him back his money. Al was drunk one night down at the Mint threatening to kill Drew." She shrugged again. "I'm sure there are more. Like Pete Ferris. Rumor was that Drew was sleeping with his wife. They almost got a divorce over it. Still might even all these years later."

"Thanks," Chloe said as Nici pushed off the bridge railing making it clear that she was done. "I'll walk you back."

"Don't bother. I know the way." Nici brushed past her but turned before exiting the bridge. "Seriously, why stick your neck out like this? Why stir this all back up? I can tell you right now Bert Calhoun isn't going to like it—not to mention Justin. So I'm not sure who you think you're going to make points with—"

"Hasn't there been a time when you did something just because it felt like the right thing to do?" Chloe asked her.

"Whatever," Nici said with a shake of her head before turning and leaving.

Chloe stood for a few moments longer on the bridge, looking down at the frozen river. Fall leaves had gotten stuck in the ice making strange dark patterns. She thought of what Nici had told her. She heard her grandmother's voice in her ear.

Best be ready for the consequences when you go poking a porcupine with a stick, missy. Someone's bound to get hurt and it won't be the porcupine.

JUSTIN'S CELL PHONE rang as he was headed into town from the Rogers Ranch. He'd spent part of the morning having breakfast and visiting with Dawson's mother, Wilhelmina. Willie was a tall, wiry ranch woman with a true heart of gold. She'd taken him in and fed him more times than he could remember.

He'd always had the feeling that she would have loved to have given his father a piece of her mind. But had hesitated because she feared that Bert would take it out on him.

He saw it was Nici calling and picked up. "Hey," he said.

"I thought I should give you a heads-up," she said. "Chloe Clementine."

Justin felt his chest tighten. "What about her?"

"You know she's an investigative reporter, right? Well, guess what she's investigating?" She didn't give him time to guess, even if he had been about to. "Drew's death."

Justin swore under his breath. "How do you know this?"

"I just went for a walk with her. She wanted to know who hated Drew enough to want him dead."

He could see the outskirts of town ahead. "What did you tell her?"

"I thought about not giving her anything," Nici said. "But then I thought, it's her funeral. So I gave her some names."

He swore again. "Who?"

"Monte Decker, Al Duncan and Pete Ferris."

"Why is Chloe doing this?" He hadn't realized he'd asked the question aloud until Nici answered.

"She says all she's after is the truth and that it's

the right thing to do. Some BS like that. But I can tell she's doing it for you."

He swore. That was the last thing he wanted.

"I thought the sheriff ruled Drew's death an accident?" Nici said.

"She did."

"So why is Chloe— She said that someone threatened her if she kept looking into Drew's death."

"It wasn't you, was it?" He had to ask.

She laughed. "No, maybe if I'd thought of it and known she was looking into Drew's death. So you didn't know."

"No, but I'll make a point of asking her what she thinks she'd doing when I see her. Thanks." He disconnected as he entered Whitehorse and headed for the house where Chloe and her sisters had grown up.

CHLOE WALKED INTO Monte Decker's office at the bank and closed the door. Monte was a forty-something rangy former Eastern Montana farm boy with a small bald spot in his short dark hair. He wasn't bad looking in his expensive suit, although as he tugged at the neck of his shirt she got the feeling he wasn't comfortable with his position. Or maybe she just had that effect on men, because he had a strangled look when he glanced up from the paperwork on his desk and saw her.

"You probably don't know me," she said as she took a seat. Other than papers strewn across his desk, there was a framed photo of Monte holding a huge walleye. From the background, it seemed he'd caught it at Nelson Reservoir. Why it caught her attention was because it was the only framed photo on his desk. No wife and kids. No favorite old dog. Just Monte and a fish.

"I'm Chloe Clementine."

"Clementine? Frannie's…"

"Granddaughter. I'm an investigative reporter."

Before that, he'd looked as if he'd expected her to ask for a loan. Now though, he leaned back and took her in, clearly speculating on why she was sitting in his office.

"What was your relationship with Drew Calhoun?"

The question startled him. He glanced out through the glass partitions that formed his office as if worried about who was watching them.

Monte began to perspire. He tugged at his collar. "What kind of question is that?"

"I know you played poker with him, that you caught him cheating and that you lost a lot of money to him."

Monte looked around as if he wanted to run. "I don't know where you got your information but I really don't have time for this. Drew is dead. Why are you asking questions about him?"

"Because I believe he was murdered and not by Justin Calhoun."

Monte opened his mouth, closed it and opened it again. "I—I thought it was an accident."

"You must have been angry when you caught him cheating," she said.

Realizing there was no place to run, he took a deep breath and said, "This really isn't the place to talk about this."

Chloe reached back and closed the door of the small glassed-in office. "Help me out here. You had reason to want Drew dead if you lost a lot of money to him and then realized he'd been cheating."

"He paid me back with interest," Monte said.

She wasn't sure she believed him, but she didn't call him on it. "So you were friends?"

The banker didn't look as if he would go that far. "We'd known each other since we were kids."

Chloe leaned toward him. "I know Drew had enemies. I'm betting there was one of them who hated him enough that they wanted him dead. If not you, then who?"

"Not me," Monte said, looking around the bank again. He swallowed, his Adam's apple bobbing up and down for a moment.

"I really appreciate your help. I don't want to stay in your office longer than is necessary. There must be someone—"

"Pete Ferris," Monte said in a hoarse whisper. "This did not come from me. If anyone hated Drew, it was Pete and with good reason after he caught Drew with his wife, Emily," he said quietly. "Now please. I need to get back to work."

"Where can I find Pete?"

JUSTIN NEVER MADE it to the Clementine place. He was a few blocks away when he spotted Chloe walking down the street. He pulled alongside and put down his window. "Hey, girl!" His earlier shock and anger at what she was doing faded as she turned in his direction. He'd seen her only in his memory since that winter kiss so long ago. If anything she was more beautiful, her cheeks glowing from the cold, her blue eyes sparkling in the frosty morning. For a moment, it took his breath away seeing her again.

She stopped walking, just stood looking at him. Her features softened, those big blue eyes warming.

"Wanna hop in?"

Chloe seemed to hesitate for only a moment before she walked over and climbed into the passenger side of his truck.

The scent of her perfume hit him like a fist. Funny how a scent could transport a person back years. Her blond hair was short now, cut in a bob that made her high cheekbones look ever higher. And those eyes…

"Damn, but you look good," he said.

She smiled then, lighting up the cab of the pickup and sending his heart drumming. "You look pretty darned good yourself."

He grinned at that. "Seems we need to talk."

"Nici." She nodded. "I figured she'd call you."

Justin shifted the pickup into gear. "Buy you lunch?"

Chapter Six

"Chloe, what are you doing?" Justin asked once they were seated at the back at Ray J's Barbecue.

She shook her head. Earlier, she'd felt alive for the first time since she'd lost her job. She'd been on an investigation and she'd known she was onto something big. Her heart had been pounding, her blood rushing. She had purpose again. She was like a hound on the scent and it felt good.

Now though, sitting here with Justin, she wasn't so sure. She didn't want to make things harder for him. Seeing him reminded her of how opening all of this up again was going to affect the one person she cared about.

"I want to clear your name," she said, thinking that was only partly true.

"Chloe, I wasn't arrested. I'm not in prison. I'm a free man. I don't need to be cleared."

"Don't you?" She glanced over her shoulder. Two couples were sitting at a table just inside the door.

They were looking in her and Justin's direction and it was clear they'd been talking about one of them.

"I don't give a damn what the locals think," he said.

She didn't believe him, but didn't argue the point. He wouldn't have left and stayed away for so long if he didn't care what people in Whitehorse thought about him. She leaned toward him. "Help me find out the truth."

"Chloe—"

"Don't you want to know what really happened that night?"

He brushed a hand through his sandy blond hair. It looked as if it had been freshly trimmed. Just like his designer stubble. But there was still a ruggedness about him. She'd fallen for a boy. This was a man across from her.

He looked strong and determined. And yet when she looked into those blue eyes, she also saw a man who'd been dragged through hell. Her heart went out to him.

She reached across the table and placed her hand over his warm one. "I'm good at my job. Between the two of us—"

He shook his head, looking sad as his blue gaze met hers. He turned his hand to cup hers in his large palm. For a moment, he looked down at their hands intertwined together. Was that regret she saw in his expression? Did she really think that they could pick up where they'd left off all those years ago?

As the waitress brought their pulled pork meals, Justin changed the subject, asking about her life since they'd last seen each other. She told him about college and the newspapers she'd worked for and even some of the stories she'd done.

"I suppose you already know my story," he said after they'd finished eating. He pushed back his plate and studied her. "I know you want to help me and I appreciate that, but that's not why I came back."

She had finished what she could eat of her meal. Her stomach had been churning from the moment Justin had pulled up next to her on the street. Seeing him again had been her dream and her fear. When she saw him sitting behind the wheel of the pickup, her heart had leaped to her throat. He was so handsome. She'd been frozen to the spot just looking at him.

The waitress came by. Chloe asked her for a go-box since she hadn't done the wonderful meal justice.

"Why did you come back?" she asked after the waitress left.

"There were people I needed to see." He smiled, his eyes crinkling. "I wanted to ask you to the New Year's Eve Masquerade Dance. That is, if you don't already have a date."

She couldn't help but smile. "I'd love to go with you." She cocked her head at him. "You aren't asking me out thinking that it will stop me from digging into Drew's death with or without your help, are you?"

She thought for a moment he would take back his invitation.

His smile faded but he chuckled and shook his head. "I doubt there is anything I could do to stop you short of hog-tying you. No, the invitation had no strings. You do what you feel you have to do, but Drew's death was an accident. A senseless tragedy."

Maybe, she thought as she studied him. *Why is it I don't think you believe that any more than I do?*

"WAS THAT JUSTIN CALHOUN?" Annabelle cried, staring out the window at the pickup pulling away as Chloe came in the door.

"I thought you were out at the Rogers Ranch with your fiancé," Chloe said.

"I was. I came back to tell you that Justin is staying at Dawson's house. But I see that you already know he's in town." Annabelle looked as if she wanted to jump up and down with excitement. "So did he ask you?"

She didn't have to ask what her sister meant. "Yes, he asked me to the dance New Year's Eve and I said yes, but then I told him I wasn't going to stop looking for Drew's killer."

Her sister's face fell. "Was that really necessary?"

"I think it is. I'm sure I'm onto something and I don't intend to stop," she said as she hung up her coat by the door.

"Are you sure this isn't about you missing your job?" Annabelle asked.

"You've been talking to TJ. By the way, where is she?"

"With Silas. They went down to Art's to pick out flooring for their house."

Annabelle rushed to her to hug her tightly. "I just feel bad for you."

"Don't. I'm fine. I'll find a job when I'm ready and—"

"I was talking about a man."

She groaned. "Please, do not start. I have a date. Isn't that enough for right now?"

Annabelle stepped back from the hug. "Unless you find out that he's a killer. It would really stink if he was in jail by New Year's Eve." Her eyes suddenly widened. "Or worse if he—"

"Justin didn't kill anyone."

"You'd better hope so if you're going to start hanging out with him. But I'd be careful. Who knows for sure what happened that night? If there is one thing I've learned, it's that people aren't always who you think they are."

JUSTIN HADN'T BEEN out to the ranch in more than five years. As he drove down the dirt road toward the Little Rockies, he was filled with so many bad memories. He tried to remember some good ones. The good ones all involved his mother. She'd died when he was fourteen. It seemed looking back that she spent what years she had with him trying to make up for the love his father didn't have for him.

Ahead he saw the ranch sprawled out in front of him, running clear to the mountains. Thousands of acres, thousands of cattle. Anyone who knew cattle knew the Calhoun Cattle Company Angus. From his great-great-grandfather to his father, each had continued the legacy—one Drew would have stepped into, had he lived. Their father had raised him to take over one day.

What was ironic about it was that his older brother hated the ranch. He felt tied down. His future had been set even before he was born and he'd resented the hell out of it. No wonder he'd been the way he was when it came to the drinking, gambling and women, Justin thought. Drew had rebelled every way he knew how. And he'd resented Justin for not being the chosen one.

Justin let out a bitter laugh. All he'd ever wanted was to take over the ranch and keep the legacy alive. He felt as if it was in his blood. He'd worked hard, hoping his father would notice. But while Bert Calhoun had cut Drew slack time and time again, he'd never given Justin the same.

As he turned down the road that lead to the main house, Justin was shocked to see that several of the fence posts had rotted and now hung from the barbed wire. He felt a jolt of anger and confusion. One thing that his father prided himself on was keeping the place up. Junk was hauled off. Nothing was left out in the pasture to rust and fall to ruin. Fences were constantly mended. Everything got a fresh coat of paint as needed. His father never left anything undone. It was that pride in what the family had built that Justin had missed the most while he'd been gone.

"We have a standard we need to keep," Bert Calhoun always said. And then would pat Drew on the back.

Justin sighed, wondering for a moment what he was doing here. The main house came into view but there was still plenty of time to turn around and leave before his father saw him. He thought of Chloe and her determination to do what she thought was right—no matter what.

He'd hoped there was some way to stop her. But her determination was something he admired in her. He did worry, though, whether she had any idea what she was getting herself involved in.

He sped on up and pulled in front of the main house. There was only one truck out front, one that he recognized, which also took him by surprise. By now his father would have had a least one new truck. He usually traded pickups every three years.

Turning off the motor, he sat for a moment. He felt as if he was getting out in the middle of the lions' den and that they hadn't been fed in a very long time. Opening his door, he stepped out. Looking at the house, he got his second surprise. It needed paint. For a moment, he wondered if his father still lived there.

But then the front door slammed open and Bert

Calhoun, a man bigger than life, stepped out holding a shotgun in both hands.

"Welcome home," Justin said under his breath.

Chapter Seven

Chloe couldn't get Justin off her mind. Why had he really come back? She hoped he wasn't planning to do anything crazy. It was clear at lunch that he had a lot on his mind. She hadn't been surprised when she'd seen him drive off in the direction of his family ranch. Since she knew he'd stayed out at the Rogers Ranch last night, she worried about what he was planning to do.

He was worried about *her*? How long it had been since he'd seen his father? What was Justin hoping would happen when he saw him? She doubted Bert Calhoun had mellowed in the past five years or even if he had fifty years. What was Justin walking into?

She knew the only thing that would keep her mind off worrying about him was continuing her investigation. It was at least one way that maybe she could help. Also she felt she'd started something she had to finish—no matter what.

Pete Ferris owned a small insurance company in downtown Whitehorse. It was early afternoon when she pushed open the door and stepped in to find the receptionist's desk empty. Past it was one large office.

Even from where she stood she could see the nameplate on the big desk. Peter Ferris. Past it was the man himself sitting behind the desk, leaning back in his large office chair, a landline phone to his ear.

A former football star at the University of Montana, Pete was a nice-looking man in his late forties who appeared as if he still worked out often.

As the door closed, a faint bell sounded. Pete looked up and was instantly wary. Had Monte got to feeling guilty and called Pete? It would appear so.

"I have to go," he said into the phone and quickly hung up. Getting to his feet, he came around the desk. "Can I help you?"

At a sound behind her, Chloe turned to see a fresh-faced young woman who couldn't have been more than twenty. She came in through the door with a stack of mail which she dropped on the receptionist's desk, then started to take off her coat.

"I think we should talk about this in private," Chloe said as she turned back to Pete. "Don't you?"

He looked as if he had been planning to throw Chloe out of his office building before his receptionist had come in. Now he reluctantly motioned her in, going behind her to say something to the young woman before he closed the door.

"What's this about?" he asked, impatiently as he took his chair again.

"I think you already know. Drew Calhoun."

Belligerently, he asked, "And what business is it of yours?"

"None. I'm an investigative reporter. I don't believe Drew's death was an accident."

"That's ridiculous," Pete snapped. "The sheriff—"

"I've already talked to the sheriff and I've seen the coroner's report."

"Then I would think that would be the end of it." He started to get up.

"I understand you had reason to want Drew dead."

He froze for a moment, before dropping back into his chair with a sigh. His face a mask of fury, he bit off each word. "This is none of your business."

"Murder is everyone's business. Your wife was having an affair with Drew. How long had you known about it?"

He pushed to his feet again. "I'm not answering your questions."

"Maybe your wife will be more forthcoming," Chloe said, rising as well.

"You are not to go near my wife," he said through gritted teeth. "If you do…"

She merely looked at him until he sat back down. She'd interviewed CEOs of big corporations, high-powered politicians, murderers and assorted criminals. An insurance man didn't scare her.

"It wasn't what everyone thought, all right?" Pete finally said.

"How is that?"

"Drew… My wife… They were just friends." He seemed at a loss for words and she felt sorry for him. No one wanted his dirty laundry hung up before a stranger. Especially a reporter.

"How long did this friendship last?" she asked.

He looked away, his jaw working. "For a couple of months."

That was the heartbreaker, she knew. When everyone in town knows but you're the last to hear. It was the trouble with small towns. But betrayal hurt no matter how many people had been talking behind your back.

"I'm sorry. How long have you been married?"

"Twenty-six years. We were high school sweethearts."

"The marriage survived?"

He met her gaze. "I didn't divorce her, if that's what you're asking. Nothing physical…happened between them. They got too close as friends. Drew became…dependent on my wife emotionally. There was no…affair. I don't expect you to believe that, but it's true."

He was the one having trouble believing it, she thought. And he also hadn't forgiven his wife. Nor had he gotten over Drew's betrayal. "You and Drew were friends?"

"We played poker together."

"I see." And she did. Nici had said she didn't think Drew had friends. "Okay, but if you didn't shoot him, then who did?"

"GET OFF MY PROPERTY!" Bert Calhoun called to Justin. "You're trespassing."

"The house needs a coat of paint," Justin said as he continued walking toward his father. "Also there are some fence posts I noticed on the way in that need to be replaced."

"You've got gall coming here and telling me what needs to be fixed," his father ground out.

"It's been five years. I think it's time we talked."

Bert raised the shotgun. "*You* think? Who do you think you are?"

"Your son."

His father shook his head. "You and I don't have anything to talk about. You're dead to me."

Justin stopped at the foot of the porch steps. "Then I guess pulling the trigger on that shotgun won't change a thing, will it? I'm not leaving until you hear me out." He planted his hands on his hips and looked up at his father.

From a distance, Bert Calhoun had looked just as big and rangy as he remembered him. But up close, his father had shrunk. He looked older than his age and not half as strong as he once was.

Drew's death had killed a part of his father. Justin could see that as clearly as day. He wanted to feel sorry for him since Bert Calhoun had put everything into his eldest son—including all his love. All the old resentments and hard feelings came to the surface like oil on water. But he refused to voice them standing out here in the snow in front of the house where he'd been raised.

He was a Calhoun, son of Bert Calhoun, and damned if he wouldn't have his say.

CHLOE FELT SORRY for Pete Ferris as she left his office. He hadn't wanted to tell her who else she should talk to.

"Isn't it time you quit covering for Drew Calhoun?" she'd asked. "Do you really owe him anything?"

He'd denied it and finally given her a name. It hadn't been one she'd expected. She'd thought it would be another one of the men Drew had played poker with.

"Tina Thomas?" she'd repeated.

"That's right," Pete Ferris had said with no small amount of apparent enjoyment. "The mayor's ex-wife."

"Ex before Drew or after?"

"After. He'd threatened to kill Drew and on more than one occasion. But the mayor didn't have it in him. Tina…well, she had reason to kill Drew and would have done it without breaking a nail."

The last made Chloe think of the scratches on Drew Calhoun presumably from a woman.

City Hall was in a brick building at the center of town, while the mayor's house was up on the hill overlooking it. The newest houses were out on the golf course or east of Whitehorse proper, past where the new hospital had gone up.

The houses on what was known as Snob Knob on the hill overlooking town were split-levels from another era. On the short walk up the hill, Chloe put in a call to her sister Annabelle. "What do you know about Tina Thomas?"

"Who?"

"The mayor's ex-wife."

"Let me make a call. I'll get right back to you."

Annabelle called back almost at once. "I just talked to Mary Sue—she is a fount of information. Tina was half Ralph's age so no one was surprised when the marriage ended. From what I heard, she's a bit snooty, thinks she's better than everyone. Shoot, that's what some people still think about me," Annabelle mused and Chloe spurred her on with a *yeah, yeah*. "Anyway, she's probably lovely and nice."

"Just misunderstood like you, right?" she laughed as she thanked Annabelle and disconnected.

Chloe felt as if she wasn't getting anywhere. Digging into Drew's past just felt dirty because all she was turning up was an assortment of women—usually someone else's. That Drew had cheated at gambling didn't feel like much of a surprise. Nor did Monte Decker seem like much of a killer, although she knew killers didn't have a certain look.

Any of Drew's addictions could have gotten him killed. But none of them felt substantial enough, although she'd heard that the number one cause of murder was a domestic dispute.

So far she hadn't heard much good about Drew.

Maybe Tina would have glowing things to say about him. Or not since Pete had said Tina had reason to want Drew dead. After climbing the steps to the front door, she rang the bell. It chimed inside the house. She waited and then rang it again.

The woman who came to the door was tall and slim with large luminous brown eyes, and close to Chloe's own age. Her long dark hair was pulled back into a low ponytail. She wore active wear though she didn't appear to be working out at the moment. But she did sound breathless as if she'd run down from upstairs.

"Can I help you?" she asked, glancing at Chloe, then out to the sidewalk as if she was looking for someone else.

Chloe suddenly had the feeling that Tina wasn't alone. "Did I catch you at a bad time?"

"No, I—I'm sorry, what do you want?"

On a hunch, Chloe said, "I'm the one who's sorry. I must have the wrong house. I was looking for... Never mind." She took a step back leaving a perplexed Tina staring after her as she walked away.

But she didn't go far. She walked partway down the hill to the park where she had a good view of the back of Tina's house and waited. The house was at the end of the street so the backyard was fairly private. It opened onto an alley that led down to the park.

Chloe cleaned snow from one of the swings and sat. She had a feeling that her stopping by had cooled whatever had been going on in the house. And it appeared she'd been right. She hadn't been waiting long when a young man wearing a baseball cap came out of the back of the mayor's house.

He kept his head down as he crossed the yard out of view of the neighbors and then turned down the alley, walking fast until he reached an older model pickup parked behind a fence on the far side of the small park.

But she still recognized him. Deputy Kelly Locke.

"You're wasting your breath," Bert Calhoun said, pointing the barrel end of the shotgun at his son as Justin climbed the steps.

He half expected his father to pull the trigger, but he wasn't backing down. He'd done too much of that in the past. As he reached the porch, he pushed the shotgun barrel aside and, opening the front door, walked into the house.

With each step, he fought memories, both bad and good. There'd been a time when he was young that his father had put a hand on his shoulder or let him climb up into his lap. But always when Drew wasn't around. But he'd never doubted that he had his mother's love and attention. If she hadn't died, maybe things would be different.

He glanced around the house, seeing that nothing had changed. Except for the need of paint and a few repairs, the place looked the same, he thought as he stopped just inside the door to wipe the snow from his boots.

Behind him, he could feel the cold rushing in. He'd left the front door open, not sure his father would follow him. He stepped in to warm himself in front of the fireplace, his back to the door. The rancher wouldn't shoot him in the back—not in the house. He wouldn't want that image on his mind every time he built a fire in the fireplace.

Behind him, he heard the door close. As he turned, he watched his father lean the shotgun against the wall by the door and hesitate a moment before crossing the living room to the bar along one wall. He watched his father make himself a drink, noticing that the elderly rancher's hands were trembling.

"I figured you'd show up eventually," Bert said as he poured himself a Scotch. He didn't offer Justin one as he brought the old-fashioned glass to his lips and took a gulp. "You know what they say about bad pennies."

"No, but I know what they say about fathers and sons," Justin said as he took off his hat and sat down. He rested the Stetson on his knee as he looked at his father. "Say what you will, but I'm your son. Your blood courses through my veins. I'm not any happier about it than you are."

His father finished his drink and set down the glass a little too hard. "Have your say and then get out."

"It's time you quit blaming me for your mistakes," Justin said. "I didn't kill Drew. I didn't like him, but then again, no one who knew him did." His father started to argue, but he cut him off. "You and I agree on one thing though. He didn't kill himself. He was too arrogant, even drunk and beaten up, to take his own life. He was also too familiar with a gun to kill himself accidentally. I've seen him a lot drunker and a lot meaner. When I found him, he looked…scared. I think you're right about someone shooting him."

"Hell yes, I am," Bert snapped. "And I know who." He glared at him with such contempt that Justin felt it down to the toes of his boots.

Why had he expected this might go differently? Nothing had changed from five years ago. His father was convinced that he was responsible for Drew's death. Drew hadn't just been the favorite. He'd been the prodigal son. With him gone, Bert Calhoun was withering up, rotting away in his grief and anger.

Justin swore under his breath as he thought of what Chloe had said. He'd wanted no part of her investigation. He'd come here to set the record straight not play detective.

"Quite frankly, I don't give a damn who killed Drew," Justin said as he glanced around the living room. "It's one reason I left and didn't come back. I didn't want to keep hearing about it. The perfect son. Dead and gone." His gaze settled again on his father. "I came out here to tell you that I am moving back and I don't care if you kept believing I killed Drew until your dying day. But seeing you, in the state you're in, in the state this ranch is in, you've left me no choice." He rose to his feet and turned to leave.

"What are you saying? You think you can just walk in here and—"

"And what?" Justin snapped, swinging around to face him again. He'd never stood up to his father before. It didn't make him feel good. But then again, he hadn't felt good about his father in a very long time. "Tell you that you look like something the dogs dragged in? That you've clearly been so busy wallowing in pity that you've let the place go? That your hate is eating you up alive? Who else is going to tell you, old man? You see anyone else around here who gives a damn?"

His father took a threatening step toward him. Justin didn't move. His father didn't come any closer. "It's none of your business," he said, but there was little strength behind his words.

"As long as my last name is Calhoun, it sure as hell is my business," Justin said. "You can say I'm dead to you, but don't kid yourself. I'm a whole lot like you and that isn't anything that makes me proud."

"If you just came out here to insult me—"

"I'm going to find out who killed your precious son," Justin said with a curse. "It's the last thing I want to do, but I don't see that I have any choice. And when I do find his killer, I'll be expecting an apology from you and damned if you won't give it to me."

With that, he turned and walked out.

BERT CALHOUN STARTED to stumble back to the bar to pour himself another drink, but changed his mind.

His heart was racing and he felt light-headed. He made his way to a chair and fell into it. He'd never thought he'd see Justin again—let alone the Justin who'd just been in his living room. It had come as a shock seeing him drive up like that.

But when his youngest son had gotten out of the pickup…

He felt weak with fury. The cold nerve. The past five years had changed Justin. He'd obviously been doing a lot of manual labor. He was bigger, stronger, more confident and self-assured than he'd ever seen his youngest.

It was a man who'd climbed out of that pickup.

He tried to swallow the lump in his throat. Justin had Mary's coloring and the same cornflower-blue eyes, unlike Drew who'd taken after him with dark hair and pale blue eyes. It had been startling to look into Justin's eyes. How could he not see Mary in their son?

And yet their oldest, Drew, had taken more after his mother in ways that hadn't done him well. He lacked ambition and drive. Mary had been sweet as sunshine, but she'd been fragile even before the cancer.

He thought about what Justin had said about being more like his father than Drew. That it was true did nothing to alleviate his anger at his son. Maybe that is what hurt the most. He saw himself in Justin when he'd wanted to see more of himself in Drew.

Shaking his head, he thought of the things Justin

had said. Hurtful, painful things. The boy had always been as stubborn as a brick wall. The man was no different. How dare he call him an old man? An old man without anyone. True or not, it wasn't right.

So now he was going to find Drew's killer? The arrogance. And demand an apology? Over his dead body.

Bert tried to catch his breath. His heart seemed to have taken off again like a wild stallion. He pressed a hand to his chest as there was a knock at the door. If it was Justin— He felt blood rush to his head at the thought, his anger making it hard for him to see let alone breathe. He tried to get to his feet, but realized he couldn't. Another knock, this one more insistent.

He tried to call out, but he couldn't get enough air to do so. Panic began to set in. He couldn't get up. He couldn't speak. What if whoever was at the door went away?

One of his hired men stuck his head in the doorway. "Mr. Calhoun?"

Bert opened his mouth but nothing came out. He held both hands over his heart, feeling as if it was trying to burst out of his chest. Justin was going to be the death of him, he thought as the hired hand rushed to his side.

"Mr. Calhoun? Mr. Calhoun!"

He watched as if from a spot on the ceiling as the man called for an ambulance and then changed his mind. "I'm bringing him in. I don't think he'll make it if we have to wait for the EMTs."

Bert observed from that misty distance as he was helped to the man's truck. He didn't remember the drive into town. He had only a vague memory of being wheeled down a white hallway and thinking he didn't want to die.

The last thing he remembered was seeing Mary and her look of disappointment before everything went black.

Chapter Eight

Justin drove back into town. He was still shaken from his visit to the ranch and seeing his father after five years. He'd expected him to be like he'd always been—a big, strong, stubborn man who handled things. Handled things not with a lot of finesse but Bert Calhoun never backed down from a challenge or a fight.

Instead, he saw weakness, something he never thought he'd see. Something he thought his father would never *let* him see. There was stubbornness and attitude, but so little to back it up.

He'd known that Drew's death had almost killed his father. But he'd expected Bert Calhoun to deal with it the way he dealt with everything at the ranch: with a stubborn resolve to succeed and go on at all costs.

But this time, it wasn't just Drew's death. He lost both sons.

That sounded like his mother's voice in his head. It definitely hadn't come from him, he thought with a curse. Drew had been *the* son. His father had always treated Justin as if he didn't matter. Drew had been his father's hope for the future. And now with Drew gone…

Justin mentally kicked himself for staying away so long. The Calhoun Cattle Company was his legacy. He hadn't realized how much his father had needed him, whether he liked it or not. He hadn't been able to stay five years ago because of his father's accusations. Bert hadn't thrown him off the ranch, but it was clear that the sight of him made the man livid.

So Justin had left. He wasn't proud of that now. He should have stayed and fought. He thought about Chloe and smiled to himself. She was one determined young woman. Nothing stopped her. But that also worried him. If they were right and Drew was murdered, then the murderer was more than likely still around.

And damned if Chloe wasn't going to stop until she found him—or her.

That's why he had to find her. He couldn't let her do this alone. It was something he should have done five years ago. Now the trail was cold.

Sadly, Drew's death was only one of the reasons he'd come back. What had lured him was the thought of Chloe Clementine. Just the sound of her voice on the phone. He shook his head. All this for a New Year's Eve dance with a woman he'd kissed once years ago? But it had been some kiss, he thought now smiling.

Justin told himself that he must be losing his mind. Was he really going looking for a killer? He didn't care what people said about him. Even his father's accusations hadn't been enough to make him want to look for the person who killed Drew. Because even five years ago he hadn't believed his death was an accident.

He'd figured Drew had infuriated the wrong person. He hadn't wanted to dig into the mess his older brother had made of his life. He still didn't. But when he'd seen the depleted shape his father was in, he *had* felt responsible. Because he'd left and hadn't looked back. No wonder his father didn't think he cared.

Justin had believed that he didn't matter because that was the way his father had treated him. The thought that he'd let himself believe that made him angry as hell. And now he'd told his father that he was going to find his brother's killer.

How was he going to do that after five years? What if he was wrong? What if Chloe was too? Maybe the sheriff was right and it had been a stupid accident. Or maybe Drew had killed himself.

As he drove over to her house, he felt sick with a mix of emotions he hadn't dealt with in five years. He'd loved his brother even as mean as Drew had been to him. Blood was blood. It would have been easier to keep driving and put Whitehorse in his rearview mirror forever.

But he was enough like the father he'd known growing up that this was one fight he wasn't going to run from. He couldn't let Bert Calhoun go on believing that his youngest son was a killer. Just as Chloe had said, it was time he cleared his name and then take Chloe to the New Year's Eve Masquerade Dance.

WHEN CHLOE TAPPED at Tina's back door, the woman rushed to open it and froze. She'd clearly been expecting the deputy who'd just left. What surprised Chloe was that Tina had rushed to the door not looking excited or expectant but angry. Had the two had a fight? Because of Chloe showing up?

"You?" Tina put her hands on her hips. "Let's have it. You a friend of his? Girlfriend? Or just a nosy neighbor?"

"I'm not here about your…friend who just left," Chloe said. "I want to talk to you about Drew Calhoun."

The woman looked surprised. "He's dead."

"That's why I need to talk to you." She stepped past into the house.

"Well, come in," Tina said sarcastically.

Chloe entered the kitchen, pulled up a chair and sat. She didn't like Tina and she was losing patience. "Coffee?"

"For real?" the woman sighed. "A cola is the best I can do since I wasn't expecting company."

Chloe thought about calling her on that, but

merely looked at her before saying, "A cola would be delightful. Thank you."

Tina put the cola can on the table. "What? You want ice?"

"I'll make this do." She opened the cola and took a drink. All this walking all over town had left her thirsty. "Tell me about you and Drew."

"That was years ago."

"At least five. When did your ex-husband find out?"

"You writing a book? What's all this to you?"

"I'm an investigative reporter."

Tina eyes widened. "If you're thinking of putting this in the newspaper—"

"I'm not. I'm investigating Drew's death for other reasons. Your ex-husband, when did he find out about you two? Months before, weeks, days?"

Tina pulled out a chair but seemed to change her mind and pushed it back in to continue standing. "A week."

"How'd he take it?"

"How do you think he took it?"

"He threatened to divorce you, kill you, kill Drew?"

"Oh, that's where you're headed," Tina sighed. "Have you met my ex-husband? I couldn't even get him to kill a spider when we were married."

"Someone beat up Drew the night he died. Was it your ex?"

"Ralph?" she laughed. "He blustered but wasn't

about to go after Drew. Drew was half his age and in much better shape." She shook her head. "Ralph wasn't going to fight a man like that."

"What about shooting him?"

Tina eyes widened. "I thought he shot himself?"

"Does your ex-husband own a gun?"

"Yes, but I thought Drew was shot with his own gun?"

"Your ex-husband knew how to use a gun, right? Where was he the night Drew died?"

"Snoring loudly next to me in our bed."

"So you could have easily snuck out and killed Drew."

The woman laughed. "Kill Drew? Why would I do that? I loved him. I would have left Ralph for him like that." She snapped her fingers. "But Drew didn't feel the same way." Tina glared at her. "If that's all…"

"You knew there were others, right?" Chloe asked.

"Seriously? Did you just come by here to make me feel bad? Ralph divorced me because of Drew. Isn't that enough?"

"Drew was two-timing you with Pete Ferris's wife."

The woman swore. "You don't get it. Drew did what Drew wanted to do."

"And it got him killed."

"Look, I've never fired a gun in my life."

"It isn't that hard to pull the trigger," Chloe said.

Tina shook her head. "You're barking up the wrong

tree. Drew was honest with me from the get-go. He told me he hadn't loved anyone since his high school sweetheart, Patsy Carter."

"Where is Patsy now?"

"She married Blaine Simpson."

Chloe heard something in the woman's voice and frowned. "Was Drew trying to get Patsy back?"

Tina looked away. "He didn't tell me he was, but I heard that he'd been out to the ranch a few times and that Blaine Simpson said if he caught him out there he'd kick his ass from here to North Dakota. Blaine's a big cowboy. In a fair fight, Blaine would have stomped Drew into the dust. What are you going to do with all of this?" Tina asked, suddenly sounding worried.

"I'm just helping a friend find out the truth about that night," Chloe said. "How long have you been seeing Kelly Locke?"

The woman looked startled for a moment before she chuckled. "Not five years if that's what you're getting at. He's a boy. I wouldn't send a boy to do a man's work." She met Chloe's gaze. "And like I said, I loved Drew. I bawled for months after he died."

The woman sighed as she pulled up a chair. She seemed to relax. It had been five years, and Tina hadn't had anyone she could talk with about Drew Chloe realized the moment the woman began to speak again.

"Drew tended to make people mad," Tina said reflectively. "Sometimes he was like an overgrown boy himself. Maybe that was the attraction." She shrugged. "He wanted what he wanted and when he didn't get it…"

"What wasn't he getting that he wanted?"

"Other than Patsy? Money. His father had put him on a strict allowance because he'd been dipping into the ranch account. He was anxious for his old man to step down so he could take over the ranch. He thought he could do a better job of running it. The thing is, even if he could have gotten Patsy back, he would have wanted someone else. Drew wasn't happy."

Chloe could see that Tina had hoped she would be the one to make the man happy. There was clearly a lot of pain there. And a part of the woman had to hate Drew. But enough to kill him?

Interesting that the golden boy wasn't quite so golden in his father's eyes if he'd been put on a strict allowance. At least Bert had been smart enough not to turn the ranch over to him. But Drew's spending had to have been a sore point between them. Even if Bert hadn't heard about his oldest son's exploits on the county grapevine, he had been forced to curb Drew's spending.

She finished her cola and got to her feet. "Thanks for talking to me."

"You aren't going to tell anyone about—"

Chloe shook her head. She wasn't going to tell anyone. "It's your secret." She could have warned Tina that secrets have a way of getting out especially in a small town. She could have also warned Tina what a louse Kelly was.

But the woman should have already known that.

Leaving, she headed back toward the main part of town just below the hill. Her list of suspects was growing. Tina had known about Pete Ferris's wife, Emily, and about Patsy Carter Simpson. Tina hadn't wanted to share Drew. He'd cost her her marriage. But, Chloe thought, remembering Kelly sneaking out Tina's back door, the woman seemed to manage with Drew gone.

She had headed down the hill from the housing development and was walking along the edge of a ditch near the park when she hit a stretch of sidewalk that hadn't been shoveled. The snow was higher than her boots and to make matters worse, the city snowplow had banked the snow up even higher the last time the road was plowed.

Chloe stepped off the curb into the plowed road. She was questioning what she'd started and what she was going to do next when she heard the roar of an engine. She started to turn, surprised that the vehicle was so close and coming so fast.

She had only an instant to make the decision. Try to get across the road to the other side of the street? Or jump into the snowbank next to her? She glanced back and caught the glint of the pickup's reinforced cattle guard bumper a moment before she dove head-long into the snowbank.

The snow was even deeper than she'd thought.

She sank into the icy cold white stuff as she heard the vehicle roar past. It was so close that the exhaust made her cough. She tried to get up in time to see the truck, suspecting it was Tina's earlier visitor.

But by the time she could get up enough to see over the snowbank, the pickup had turned the corner and disappeared, leaving her cold and shaken from the near miss. She got to her feet, looking after the truck, as she brushed at the snow covering her clothing. Had the driver purposely put her in the snowbank to scare her? Or worse?

What if she hadn't leaped out of the way when she had?

The driver would have hit her and no one would have seen it, she realized as she looked around the area. Whoever had been driving that pickup had been waiting for her. Deputy Kelly Locke?

Chapter Nine

Justin couldn't believe what he was seeing. He'd tried Chloe's house, and finding no one around, had kept looking for her. By chance, he'd seen a truck speed by and noticed a woman climbing out of a snowbank.

He drove over to find Chloe standing at the edge of the road covered with snow. His first thought was that she must have fallen down. He glanced around. What had she been doing in this part of town? He felt his heart drop. What else, looking for Drew's killer by herself.

He swore as he watched her brush snow from her pants and shake out her gloves. Pulling up next to her, he whirred down the passenger side window. "Are you all right?"

She smiled when she saw him, loosening something in his chest. "I am now."

"Climb in," he said.

"You're on."

He reached over and opened the door. She slid in

looking like a snowman. Snowwoman. All woman even bundled up the way she was. "What happened?"

She hesitated. "I'm afraid someone just tried to run me down." He listened with growing shock and worry as she told him about the pickup truck. "If I hadn't jumped off the road when I did…"

"If I didn't know what you were up to, I'd say it was just kids," Justin said. "But since I do know, you need to go to the sheriff."

She shook her head. "I didn't get a good look at the truck. Dark and dirty won't cut it. Also I suspect the driver was just trying to warn me off. Hit and run isn't the most effective way to eliminate someone."

He heard something in her voice. She was scared. She should be. He thought about the look in his brother's eyes the night he found him. If Drew had been afraid of his killer… "Chloe, you have to stop this."

"Now I definitely can't. This started out because I wanted to find out the truth for you and admittedly being between jobs, I was feeling antsy. Now it is clear that someone thinks I'm getting too close to what really happened that night. Also it's become personal," she said as she looked down at the snow still clinging to her clothing.

He groaned as he shifted the truck into gear. "What were you doing in this neighborhood anyway?"

"Talking to the mayor's ex-wife, Tina Thomas. Did you know about her and Drew?" His expression must have given him away. "She said she loved him but Drew wouldn't commit. She also said she's never shot a gun. But I'm definitely keeping her on my suspect list."

"I don't like the feeling that you're enjoying this—even after almost being killed."

"Don't worry. I have no desire to die. I'll just be more careful next time. But I won't be scared off."

"If your plan is to track down all of Drew's women, then your suspect list is going to get awfully long."

"Just the ones who either personally have reason to have wanted him dead—or their husbands who were maybe even more motivated to see Drew gone," Chloe said.

"We're both probably wrong about him being murdered. The sheriff—"

"Nice try, but I ask a few questions around town and someone calls me and tells me to quit or I'll regret it. Now someone tries to run me down. We aren't wrong and you know it."

"I thought you said the driver was only trying to warn you off?" He had her there. "Chloe, just because someone has something they want to keep secret, it doesn't mean they murdered Drew. What it proves is that you digging into all of this is dangerous. Is there anything I can say to make you stop?"

She gave him an impatient look. "Hopefully, you know me better than that. I'm onto something. One of Drew's enemies is going to make a mistake. I must be getting close. These are the kinds of secrets that are bound to come out."

"If we're right, then the killer has gotten away with murder for five years."

Chloe smiled. "Exactly. The person felt safe and now they don't. The more I rattle their cage—"

Justin swore. "Then we'll do it together."

CHLOE LOOKED OVER at him in surprise as he turned down her street. Isn't this what she'd hoped for? "What changed your mind? I thought you wanted nothing to do with this?"

"I don't but I have no choice. I can't have you doing this alone."

She gave him a look that said she suspected there was more to his decision.

He sighed. "I paid my father a visit."

She could tell by his expression but still she had to ask— "How did that go?"

He shook his head. "I didn't realize how badly he needed to know the truth about that night. I guess I thought after all this time... But you're right. I can't have this hanging over my head or my father's any longer." He pulled up in front of her house and cut the engine.

"Why did your sisters call me?" Justin asked turning to her.

The sudden U-turn in the conversation took her by surprise. But it was the look in his blue eyes that froze her tongue. She swallowed, almost afraid to

speak for fear of what might come out of her mouth.
She'd wanted this, needed this. Her sisters were trying to give her what could have been. How did she
explain that she'd lived all these years with a fantasy
and all because of one winter kiss?

"They knew I liked you, you know—back before
I left for college," she said.

He met her gaze and held it. "So why didn't you
keep in touch? Or maybe even come back in the
summer?"

She shook her head, hating to admit the truth for
fear of just how silly this all was. One kiss. She'd
lived off it all these years because it had been so
perfect. Or at least in her memory. "I was afraid."

"Afraid?"

"Afraid it wasn't anything. That maybe I misread
the kiss, that…" She shrugged as she looked into his
handsome face. This cowboy had been in her dreams
for years and now here he was in the flesh. Could
real life live up to the fantasy Justin Calhoun? She
thought it just might.

"Do you even remember the kiss?"

He held her gaze. "What do you think?"

She swallowed again and had to look away. "We
were so young."

"You think that makes a difference?"

"I don't know." She turned back to him. "What
do you think?"

"That we might have to test it."

His cell phone buzzed. He held up a finger and

pulled out his phone. She saw his expression change before he disconnected. "My father's in the hospital. I have to go. I'm sorry, but this discussion isn't over."

"I hope your father's all right," she said as she climbed out.

"I'll call you." And he was gone.

Chloe stood on the shoveled sidewalk watching his pickup take the corner and disappear. Her heart was pounding. She was still scared. The thought of kissing Justin again... What if they were both wrong and whatever they'd felt was no longer there?

It would be like learning there was no Santa Claus. Only worse, she thought as she noticed her sister's SUV was gone. Also there were no lights on in the house. Both sisters were probably with their significant others.

Chloe hugged herself, not sure what to do next.

THE MOMENT JUSTIN walked into the hospital on the east end of the small Western town, he saw Nici. "I got your text. How is he?"

"The doctor was waiting to talk to you," she said and gave him a hug. "When my sister called..." She pulled back to look at him. "I thought you'd want to know he'd been brought in."

He'd forgotten that Nici's older sister was a nurse's aide. "Thanks." They moved into the small waiting room, but he couldn't sit down. He was too anxious. "This is all my fault. I went out to see him. I said some things…" He swore under his breath and couldn't go on.

Nici placed a hand on his back. "This is not your fault. Your father hasn't been well for years and we both know why."

He turned to look at her. "Me."

"Not you," she said. "Drew."

"I know that for my father losing Drew was even worse than losing my mother. But the fact that he thinks I killed my own brother…"

"He just wants someone to blame other than himself for the way Drew was and how it had ended."

Justin knew that only too well. He kept seeing himself rushing into his brother's cabin, reliving the shock of seeing his brother fumbling with the gun, his hands covered in blood. He'd thought Drew had shot himself and was trying to finish the job. Acting on instinct, he'd rushed him and taken the gun from his hands. Drew had been looking at him with so much fear in his gaze. Had he known he was dying? Or was he afraid that whoever had shot him would finish the job?

Justin had fumbled his phone from his pocket with his free hand, still holding that bloody damned gun. There hadn't been a place to put it down since his brother had been sitting in the middle of the room in a chair as if watching the door…

His father had rushed in. Of course he'd thought what any sane person would have thought under the circumstances. That the man holding the gun was the killer.

"So you saw Chloe?" Nici asked as she plopped down in one of the waiting room chairs. "All that old chemistry still there?"

He looked at his friend, hearing the jealousy in her voice. But he was glad to talk about anything to keep his mind off Drew and his father lying in a hospital bed down the hall.

"Who are you dating now?" he asked, not about to talk to Nici about that kiss he and Chloe had shared.

She shook her head. "I'll take that as a yes. You don't remember telling me about the kiss, do you?" she laughed. "I'd never seen you looking so happy."

"I shouldn't have shared that with you, but you were my closest friend."

Nici nodded and gave him a sad smile. "Still am."

At a sound from the doorway, they both turned to see the doctor standing there. "Are you Mr. Calhoun's son?"

Justin quickly stepped toward him. "How is my father?"

"It's his heart," the doctor said. "He's stable now. If you want to see him—"

"No," he said too quickly making the doctor lift a brow. He didn't want to explain that he was the one responsible for his father's heart attack. He was just relieved he hadn't killed the man. "He should get some rest. I'll see him later."

Chapter Ten

Chloe was too antsy to hang out in the house alone. She couldn't quit thinking about Justin and what she'd learned. But she also hadn't forgotten the sound of that pickup's motor revved up and right behind her. She promised herself she would be more careful as she headed for Pete Ferris's house.

His wife, Emily, answered the door in an apron, her round face flushed. It surprised Chloe that she was nothing like the mayor's ex-wife. For some reason, she thought they would be more alike. She was short, plump and pretty. Apparently Drew hadn't had a type.

"Come in," the woman said, wiping her hands on the apron. "I'm baking." She turned on her heel. Chloe followed her through the living room to the large farmhouse-style kitchen.

"Help yourself," Emily said, motioning to the cookies cooling on the breakfast bar. She picked up a hot pad, opened the oven and pulled out another large batch of cookies. Chloe raised a brow at the number of cookies the woman was baking. "I donate them to the senior center," she said, seeing Chloe's questioning look.

She put the pan down and turned off the oven, tossing the hot pad aside. "You must be Chloe Clementine. Pete told me you would be stopping by." She didn't sound upset as she wiped her brow with her blouse sleeve.

"Then he told you I'm trying to find out who killed Drew. Forgive me but you don't seem the type who would fall for a man like Drew."

"Who says I fell for him?" She picked up a cookie and took a bite. She seemed to be judging the cookie. It appeared to have passed her taste test.

"Something was going on with you and Drew."

Emily laughed. "I didn't sleep with Drew."

Chloe lifted a brow. "Is that really what your husband believes?"

"My husband caught Drew over here a few times. He just assumed and so did everyone else, I guess." She shrugged. "That's their problem."

Confused, she asked, "I'm trying to find out more about Drew and what was going on with him so I have some idea who might have wanted him dead."

Emily seemed to consider this. "I'm not sure who you've talked to, but I suspect you've heard disturbing things about Drew. That wasn't the man I knew."

"If you weren't sleeping with him…"

"Don't get me wrong. He came on to me at first. I might not look like his other women, but Drew wasn't choosy. I turned him down flat and offered him a cookie."

"And he was fine with that."

"Actually no, he said he could do better and that I should be grateful he even wanted to sleep with me."

Chloe raised a brow. "And you still offered him a cookie?"

Emily smiled. "He didn't take rejection well. But under that callous facade I saw a man in pain. From then on, he'd stopped by to talk. He knew what days I baked so he'd just show up. He'd sit where you're sitting." Her voice broke.

"You cared about him."

Emily met her gaze. "There was good in him. Unfortunately, few people got to see it. He didn't let many people in."

"But he let you in. His brother thinks he was in some kind of trouble."

"He was struggling," the woman said with a nod. "His father had such high expectations of him and he hated that he was the clear favorite. He didn't understand why his brother didn't hate him, hate him *and* his father. Being held up like that was hard on him. It made him rebel."

"The gambling?"

"That and the women. I think he was looking for someone to punish him. He felt he deserved it."

"Who beat him up the night he died?"

Emily shook her head. "This is the first I've heard about it."

"Pete?"

"I highly doubt that. Pete might have threatened him, but use his fists?" She shook her head. "Drew and I had a connection. Pete resents it more than if I had slept with Drew." She shrugged. "I've tried to explain it to him."

"Did he resent it enough to want to kill Drew?"

Emily began to take the cookies off the pan and stack them with the others as if thinking about that—or stalling. "You're asking if Pete has an alibi for that night. I could tell you he was with me."

"But he wasn't. Where was he?"

The woman looked up. "I have no idea. He told me he was driving around thinking. You should take some cookies to your sisters," Emily said, reaching into a drawer to pull out a plastic bag. "I have plenty."

JUSTIN LEFT THE HOSPITAL, relieved and yet still shaken. His father had suffered a heart attack. He thought of the things he'd said to the man and felt ashamed. He'd let the past and his disappointment get to him and regretted it deeply.

There seemed to be only one way to make it up to him. Finding out the truth about Drew. But what if the truth was enough to kill his father?

He felt torn as he drove back to the center of town. At the sound of a blaring horn, his head jerked up. In the rearview mirror, he saw a pickup truck riding his tailgate. The driver wore a cowboy hat. Justin couldn't see the man's face. But from the continuing blare of the horn, he got the impression the cowboy wanted him to pull over.

Turning into an empty space along the main street, he parked and got out. Whatever this was about, he planned to put an end to it quickly. The driver of the pickup had pulled in behind him and was now opening his door.

It wasn't until he was almost to the cowboy that Justin recognized CJ Hanson, his brother's best friend. CJ shoved back his Stetson as Justin approached.

"I heard you were back but I couldn't believe it," CJ said. "I told everyone that you wouldn't have the nerve to ever show your face around here again."

CJ had played football for the Montana State University Bobcats but had flunked out after his freshman year. He'd intimidated Justin when he was younger. That wasn't the case anymore since they now stood about the same height. While CJ had gone to seed, Justin had spent years doing physical ranch work.

As he closed the distance between him and CJ, he saw the man's eyes widen in alarm. The cowboy was used to Justin being young and a little afraid of him. Seeing that he wasn't, CJ took a step back, banging into the side of his pickup.

"It sounds like you don't know what you were talking about," Justin said, getting into the cowboy's face. "I'm back and I'm staying." He wasn't sure that was even true. "If you have a problem with that, then let's settle it right now."

CJ wet his lips and took a swing at him, but being pinned against the side of his truck, the blow had little force to it. Justin blocked it easily and punched the cowboy in the face hoping to finish this quickly. The last thing he wanted was a knock-down-and-drag-out fight on the main street of town.

He heard CJ's nose break. Blood splattered over the cowboy's face. Justin took a step back, ready for CJ if he charged. But instead of barreling at him like an angry bull, the cowboy grabbed his bleeding nose with both hands and leaned back against his pickup again.

"You sucker punched me," CJ said, sounding like he had a bad cold.

Justin shook his head. "I can understand why you and my brother were best friends. That's the kind of bull he would have said. Whatever problem you have with me, I'm not going to be so easy on you next time."

With that he turned and walked away, half expecting the cowboy to ambush him from behind. No, he thought, CJ would wait for another time when he had more of an element of surprise—and a couple of friends to back him up.

The one thing Justin could be assured of was that this wasn't over. He'd better watch his back because his brother's old friend would be lying for him now.

WALKING THROUGH THE winter wonderland that was Whitehorse, Montana, in December, Chloe was trying to make sense out of what she'd learned about Drew Calhoun when her phone rang. She saw it was Justin and picked up.

"Where are you?" he asked without preamble.

"A few blocks from home. How is your father?"

"Stable after having a heart attack. I could use a drink," he said.

Without hesitation, she said, "Just tell me where to meet you."

He'd taken a table by the fireplace at the Great Northern. Only a few locals were at the bar at the other end of the room. Justin rose to pull out a chair for her and help her off with her coat. She could see that he was upset even though his father being stable had to be good news.

She was trying to read him, when she noticed the skinned knuckles of his right hand. "Eventful afternoon?"

He followed her gaze to his hand. Closed it into a fist and then straightened his fingers painfully, all the time looking sheepish. "Ran into an old friend of my brother's, CJ Hanson."

"He sounds charming."

"He was cuter before he got his nose broken, but I don't want to talk about him. What have you been up to?" He rested his elbows on the table and leaned toward her. The heat of the fireplace next to them was nothing like that in his blue eyes.

"I paid Emily Ferris a visit," she said. "It was less volatile than your visit with CJ apparently. She fed me cookies and told me about her relationship with your brother."

He leaned back as their drinks were served and didn't speak until the bartender left. "Glad to hear you took my advice."

"Justin, I told you I wasn't quitting."

Nodding, he said, "I know but from this point on, we only do this together, agreed? You investigating this alone is too dangerous."

"I didn't have to break anyone's nose," she pointed out.

He chuckled at that. "Believe me, it could have been worse." He picked up his beer and took a drink, studying her. "I mean it. I'm worried about you."

She felt heat warm her face and had to look away. This wasn't the place to be making eyes at each other. At the other end of the bar, several of the locals had noticed them. "So what's our next move?"

He grinned. "I know what I'd like mine to be."

"We're still talking about finding your brother's killer…right?"

JUSTIN WANTED TO lose himself in Chloe's blue eyes and forget everything else. He ached to kiss her again to prove to her that the chemistry was still there, only stronger. But a part of him feared that he might be wrong. He wasn't ready to take that chance yet.

"What do you suggest we do next?" he asked, sitting back as he took another drink of his beer.

Chloe shook her head. "If we could find out who beat up Drew the day he died, I think that would be a start." She told him what she'd learned about Drew from Tina and Emily. "Tina led me to believe that Blaine Simpson could be the one who beat up Drew that night. Apparently Drew was trying to get his old girlfriend—"

"Patsy Carter," Justin said with a curse. "What was Drew thinking? Blaine is a huge guy and one a man wouldn't want to mess with. Anyway, Drew and Patsy? That dog don't hunt. She broke up with him because he was cheating on her."

"It doesn't seem to me that the person who beat up your brother would be the same one who ended up shooting him."

Justin agreed. "If it had been Blaine and his intent was to kill Drew, he could have. But my brother had to know he was in danger. Why else did he have his gun out?"

Chloe shook her head. She was beautiful in the firelight. His heart beat a little faster just looking at her. "So who? The coroner's report mentioned the scratches on him. That sounds like a woman."

He thought of Nici. He wouldn't have put it past her to have literally torn into his brother that night. But for the time being, he didn't want to bring up her name. All his instincts told him that Nici would be a wildcat when she was mad, but she was no killer.

"My money is on Pete Ferris," he said. "The guy has a hell of a temper as I recall. I witnessed an argument he had with Drew a few days before my brother's death."

"Emily swears there was nothing physical between her and Drew," she said.

Justin thought about how angry Pete had been. "Do you believe her?"

"They were definitely involved emotionally. Whether she realizes it or not, she was in love with him, probably still is. I'm sure that's why her husband is so angry still. Sometimes the emotional connection is more intimate than even the physical."

He knew that to be true. He'd never forgotten Chloe after one kiss. While there'd been other women over the years who he'd had sex with, he couldn't even call up one of their faces at the moment.

"Truthfully, I have no idea where to begin to find my brother's killer—if we're right and he was murdered."

"What do you remember from back then?"

He shrugged. "Drew and I didn't travel in the same circles. I was busy much of the time doing the chores on the ranch that my brother didn't want to do and staying clear of my father."

"But you must have suspected or heard about things your brother was involved in. Did you know he gambled?"

He nodded. "There were rumors. I suspected he was in deep financially. He got involved in shady things and often had to go to our father for money. I know he owed someone money in the days before he died. Our father had cut him off financially and he was really furious over it. I could tell he was in trouble, but then again, he was often in trouble."

"But this time are we talking about someone who would kill him if he didn't pay?"

"I can't imagine we have loan sharks in White-horse," he said, but realized he knew little of the kind of people his brother had associated with. "You know, this might be a good time to go out to the ranch. Before I left, my father had boarded up Drew's cabin, leaving it just as it was the night he died. I haven't been in it since then. Maybe there's something that the sheriff missed because she didn't know Drew like I did."

Chapter Eleven

Justin seemed lost in his own thoughts on the drive out to the ranch. Chloe leaned back in the seat and watched the winter landscape blur past. At each ranch or farmhouse that they passed she would see Christmas decorations. One barn had a huge star that could be seen for miles. Another had a silhouette of the manger scene cut out of metal.

When he turned down the road to the Calhoun Cattle Company, she realized she'd never been out here before. She and Justin hadn't gotten that far in their…budding relationship. Now she realized that Justin would probably have never brought her home to meet his father and brother. She'd had no idea the extent of the animosity between the brothers. She knew that Drew had been the favorite and that had no doubt pitted the brothers against each other. Also that Justin felt devalued by his father. So much so that Bert Calhoun could believe that his youngest son was a murderer.

Justin drove on past the main house down a narrow snowy path that ended in front of a small cabin. She couldn't help but look back, seeing the tracks in the snow. He followed her gaze.

"It won't make any difference. Once I remove the boards on the door to my brother's cabin and go inside, he'll know. He boarded it up himself, saying it was never to be opened again. Anyway, he won't be getting out of the hospital for a while. Maybe we'll know something more before then."

Chloe hoped that was true, otherwise his relationship with his father would be even more strained. After getting out, Justin reached into the back of his pickup's toolbox and pulled out a crowbar. His handsome face was drawn in a look of determination. After this, there was no going back and they both knew it.

Earlier, the day had been clear, the winter sun not exactly warm but no way as cold as now. With the sun down, the temperature had dropped leaving the sky cloudy and gray. There was a dismal feeling to the evening that made Chloe even more nervous. She knew Justin wasn't looking forward to going back into this cabin. This is where he found his brother dying.

It made it all the more tense because they might get caught by one of the ranch employees or worse, the ranch manager, Thane Zimmerman. Annabelle had already warned her about him. *Big, nasty, spends a lot of time in town at the bars where he gets into fights.*

What if they got caught here? She shivered, hugging herself against the cold and worry, as she watched Justin go to work. Nails had been pounded into the walls next to the door to hold the large sheet of plywood blocking the entrance. As Justin began prying the plywood up, the nails screamed in protest.

Chloe kept looking in the direction of the main house and the other cabins. A cold breeze moved restlessly through the fallen snow, the landscape looking all the more bleak. Nearby, several horses trotted over to the fence to watch, their breaths coming out in clouds of frosty white.

The plywood came off in a loud pop before it dropped to the ground. Justin tossed the crowbar back into his pickup's toolbox, then moved the piece of plywood aside before he reached for the doorknob.

She saw him hesitate and realized how hard this must be on him. He probably hadn't been back here since that night when he heard the gunshots and came running. That he was about to relive it all again broke her heart. She put a hand on his shoulder for a moment, unable to imagine how horrible it had been to find his brother like that. Even if they hadn't gotten along.

Justin reached back and squeezed her hand before he turned the knob and the door swung open. With the cabin being closed up five years ago, Chloe had no idea what it would be like inside after all that time.

To her surprise, the scents that rushed out re-

minded her only of old musty things. Justin turned
on a light and stood in the doorway for a moment before he stepped inside. She followed. He had stopped
in the center of the room. He was staring at the chair
where according to the coroner's report his brother
had been sitting when he'd found him. There was
a stain on the chair and the floor, both now faded
and no longer resembling blood. But both of them
knew anyway.

THE CABIN WAS icy cold. Justin had been terrified to
open that door, afraid he would see his brother sitting
there fumbling with the gun. Instead, as he turned
on the light all he saw was the old cabin where his
brother did the things he didn't want their father to
know about. This was where he brought his women.
This is where he drank to excess. This is where he
occasionally brought his friend CJ so the two of them
could watch football games, drink and get loud.

What struck him most was how little his brother
had accumulated when it came to creature comforts.
If he wanted those, he could just go over to the main
house and yet Drew had spent most of his time here
except for meals.

The cabin held only the essentials: a bed, a dresser,
a couple of chairs and a television. There was a small
closet and bathroom. The cabin had allowed Drew
to come and go without their father knowing. With a
back road off the ranch, anyone visiting Drew could

park just over the hill and no one would be the wiser that they'd been on the ranch.

Is that what his killer had done that night?

There were a half dozen empty beer bottles next to the bed and a bottle of whiskey with the cap lying on the wood floor. It was hard to tell how much Drew had consumed of it since it would have evaporated over the years and now just had a dark stain at the bottom. It was the other dark stains on the chair and the floor in front of it that he tried not to look at.

He shifted his gaze to the dresser and then stepped to the bathroom. Out of the corner of his eye, he saw Chloe move to the closet and begin going through the clothes there. As she searched pockets, he opened the medicine cabinet. There was a razor, shaving cream and ibuprofen. Other than a toilet, there was a small shower. He pulled back the shower curtain. Nothing of interest.

His brother's life hadn't been here on the ranch. Drew had spent as little time as possible out here even though their father had wanted him to be the one to take over someday. If anything, Drew felt put-upon whenever the ranch was brought up at one of their meals. His brother would keep his head down, shoveling in his food and then getting up and saying he had something he had to do and leave.

He's just sowing his oats, their father used to say when Drew would drive off the ranch in a cloud of dust. *One of these days, he'll be ready to take the reins.*

Justin stepped out of the bathroom, hating the memories that flooded him, threatening to drown him. "Find anything?"

She shook her head as she stood in the middle of the room frowning. "Was the door open that night?"

He nodded and glanced toward the door, now standing open. He could see beyond it. It was darker outside than when they'd entered the cabin—but not nearly as dark as it had been that night. No moon. One of those summer nights that the air was hot and close. Not like this cold winter evening.

"You heard shots. Two close together?"

Justin shook his head. "One and then a few moments before the next one."

"You ran from the house?"

"From the horse barn."

"You could tell where the shots were coming from?"

He frowned. Why hadn't he run toward the house or one of the other cabins? In his mind's eye he saw the scene as he'd stepped from the barn. He'd seen Nici leaving, heard her vehicle, as he ran toward his brother's cabin, knowing that was where she'd come from.

"I guess I just knew that's where the shots had come from," he said, hating that he was still keeping Nici out of this. Earlier in the day, he had walked past Drew's cabin. The dust hadn't completely settled around his brother's pickup. He remembered hearing the tick of the engine as it cooled. Had Drew been alone? Or was Nici already in there with him?

Or was someone else?

CHLOE SAW THE pained look on Justin's face as he remembered—possibly more than he'd even told the sheriff.

"I ran by his pickup and came around the corner of the cabin. The door was open. Drew was in that chair."

"Facing the open door."

"He was trying to hang on to the gun. His hands were covered with blood. There was blood everywhere." His voice broke.

"He was trying to fire the gun again?"

He nodded. "At least that's what I thought. I rushed to him thinking he'd shot himself and was trying to finish the job. I took the gun away from him."

"Did he say anything? Try to speak?"

Justin was staring at the empty chair. "He…he opened his mouth, but nothing came out but a stream of blood. Then his gaze went to the door. I'm not sure what he expected to see, but he looked terrified."

"How long before your father came in?"

He shook his head. "I was trying to get my phone out to call 911 but I had the gun in one hand and the blood was so slippery… After that…" He looked up at her. "It all happened so fast. I just remember being panicked and confused. I didn't understand what had happened—just that it was very bad."

"What did your father do?"

"That part is a blur. He came rushing in and saw me holding the gun and thought I'd shot Drew. He ran to my brother and tried to stop the bleeding while screaming at me to call for help. That's all I remember."

"What about the gun? You said you were holding it when your father came in?"

"I finally walked over and set it down on the table so I could make the call. I just remember shaking so hard—and the blood... My father was crying, telling Drew to hold on, that help was coming, but I could see that my brother was gone. Then the ambulance came and the sheriff, they took us outside. The coroner came. I was standing out by that tree out there when they wheeled Drew out in the body bag. My father was hysterical by then." He took a breath and stepped outside the cabin as if he couldn't breathe.

Chloe looked around the cabin again. The light was gone in the winter sky, darkness dropping like a blanket over them even though it wasn't quite five in the afternoon. She could see Justin standing outside in the cold and dark. He appeared to be fighting to breathe.

Wanting to give him a few minutes alone, she moved around the cabin. It felt even colder in here than outside. She had little desire to spend any more time inside. But she could tell Justin needed to be alone. She finally sat down on the corner of the bed and wondered what Drew had been thinking, sitting in that nearby chair staring out past the open doorway.

She glanced in that direction, wondering what he saw, what he was afraid of seeing. As she started to rise, she saw something glitter against the baseboard between the wall and the chest of drawers. She pushed off the bed and walked over, losing sight of whatever it was. She was also losing interest, wanting to leave before one of the ranch hands caught them there.

Chloe told herself it probably wasn't anything. Maybe the silver tab from a beer can or a piece of trash. But as she peered around the edge of the bureau, she saw what looked like a small silver star. It was tarnished and looked old, but the chain attached to it still glittered as she pulled it out from the crack between the old wood flooring and the baseboard.

Her curiosity piqued now, she had to get down on her hands and knees to reach back into the crack between the wall and the bureau to pry it out.

"Chloe?" Justin said from the door.

She held up the bracelet she'd found as she got to her feet. She'd assumed they wouldn't find anything since the sheriff had no doubt searched the cabin. She'd read in the report that they'd fingerprinted the entire cabin, including the beer cans and whiskey bottle, but had only found Drew's prints.

If someone else had been in the cabin that night, they hadn't had anything to drink.

Once ruled an accidental death, there would be no reason to do more than a cursory search. Otherwise, they would have found this bracelet.

"Ever see it before?" she asked as she held it up.

JUSTIN TOOK THE delicate silver bracelet from her. A tiny star hung from the chain along with a minia-ture silver horseshoe and a heart. He held it up to the light. "The heart is inscribed." His eyes widened as he read first the name on the front, then the one on the back. He swore as his gaze met Chloe's.

"It's the bracelet Drew gave Patsy Carter," he said. "She was his high school girlfriend." Frowning, he said, "What was it doing here? Drew didn't move into this cabin until after he flunked out of college. Even if Patsy had given it back to him when she broke up with him... What would it be doing here?"

"Your brother was allegedly trying to get Patsy back. Maybe he'd tried to give it to her again. Or maybe she'd kept it after they broke up."

Justin groaned and shook his head. "Either way, if her husband found it... But it doesn't explain how it ended up in this cabin."

"We're going to have to talk to Patsy and Blaine. I understand he's a big cowboy who doesn't take kindly to anyone coming after his wife," Chloe said.

Justin nodded, dreading this. "Let's get out of here." He turned off the cabin light and closed the door. If he had his way, he'd burn this cabin to the ground. He definitely didn't think it helped his father by keeping it as some kind of shrine to Drew. Nor did he see any way to right the wrongs his brother had done.

All he could hope for was to get some closure for his father. For himself. But digging into the muck that had been his brother's life made him sick to his stomach. Drew had left a trail of hate behind him along with a lot of hurt people. Knocking on doors and asking those people if they hated Drew bad enough to kill him was the last thing he wanted to be doing any time, let alone over the holidays.

Worse, now Chloe was right in the middle of this whether he liked it or not. He glanced over at her as they climbed back into his truck. After starting the engine, he let it run for a moment to allow the heater to warm up the cab. He knew he was stalling. He'd had about all he could take of this for one day.

"It's late. I'm thinking we should put this off until tomorrow," he said. "I need to go by the hospital and check on my father."

"I probably should check in with my sisters. They're talking about a double wedding on New Year's Day."

"A double wedding, huh?"

"I guess I'm giving them away," she said with a laugh. But he could tell it wasn't easy being the oldest while her two younger sisters were getting married.

"You ever think about getting married?"

She shot him a look. "Why would you ask me that?"

"It just seems that you've been more interested in a career, that's all."

Chloe looked away. "I was. I still love what I do, but yes, I've thought about marriage, kids, a house," she laughed. "I miss baking."

He smiled over at her. "You bake?"

"I used to," she said, turning to smile at him.

"All that seems so far away from what we have been doing, doesn't it?"

She nodded. "Once we figure this out…"

"Sure." He put the pickup into gear and pulled out of the ranch. She was quiet all the way back into town. When he reached her grandmother's house, he saw that there was an SUV parked in the drive and lights on inside. "Looks like your sisters are back."

"I don't want you going out to talk to Blaine alone," she said as she reached for the door handle.

"Chloe—"

"No. I'm going with you. I want to talk to Patsy. She might tell me what she wouldn't you."

He thought she was right about that. "Okay. Nine in the morning. I'll pick you up."

"We will get to the bottom of this," she said.

Justin tried to smile. She reached over and touched his cheek. "I know how hard this is on you. It will get better."

"I hope you're right about that. But Chloe, we're looking for a killer. By now, that person knows. Next time, that truck that tried to run you down may not miss."

"So it's a good thing we're doing this together. What are the chances he'll hit both of us?" She climbed out of the pickup saying, "See you in the morning."

He watched her until she disappeared inside the house, not liking the odds. They didn't have any idea who they were looking for while the killer probably already had them in his sights.

Chapter Twelve

He was dead. Then the room came into focus. He blinked at the nurse by his bed.

"Mr. Calhoun," she said, seeing that he was trying to speak. "You've had a heart attack but you are fine now." She held up a cup of water, touching the end of the straw to his lips. He drank, wanting more, but she pulled it back, saying he could have more later.

"Drew?"

"You try to rest. The doctor will be by to see you soon. He can answer any questions you might have."

He watched her leave, his eyelids heavy, his mind sluggish. Where was Mary? He'd had a heart attack and his wife wasn't here? He closed his eyes. Justin.

A memory tried to surface but remained out of his reach. Something had happened. That much he knew and it was more than his having a heart attack. Where was his family?

The next time he opened his eyes, Justin was asleep in the chair next to his bed. He stared at his youngest son. When had he grown into a man? It felt as if he'd been in this bed for years, years he'd now lost with no memory. That thought had him aching with regret.

Justin stirred. Bert closed his eyes and pretended to be asleep as he heard his son rise. A moment later Justin touched his hand. He could feel him standing there as if unsure what to say.

"I'm sorry, Dad. So sorry."

He was wondering what Justin had to be sorry about as he heard him leave. Whatever it was, it might explain why he hadn't wanted to face his son just then. Sleep took him again, this time into a dark place that he feared was the end.

Bert heard people rushing around him. He felt something cold on his chest and a terrible jolt before nothing at all.

Chapter Thirteen

Justin woke with a headache the next morning. The day was cold and clear but he'd heard last night on the radio that a storm was coming. He'd almost reached the Rogers Ranch last night after stopping by the hospital when he got the call about his father's second heart attack. He'd thought about turning around and going back to the hospital, but worried that he'd been the one to bring it on. Maybe the best thing he could do was stay away.

The nurse had assured him that his father was stable again and that he could see him in the morning. He'd driven out to the ranch where he and Dawson had dinner, then sat around and talked over a beer until late.

When he'd picked up Chloe this morning in town, she'd looked like she'd had a long night, as well. "You up late too?"

She'd nodded. "I couldn't sleep. How was your father?"

"He had another heart attack, but he's stable

again." He couldn't fight the feeling that he was racing against a clock now. Though would finding out who'd killed Drew help his father or kill him? He had to believe that Bert Calhoun needed this. Justin just had to find the answers and soon. Another heart attack might be his father's last.

Blaine and Patsy Simpson lived ten miles out of town on a ranch not far from the Canadian border. The ranch had been in the family for several generations much like the Calhoun Cattle Company.

As they drove up, Justin spotted Blaine out by the barn. He parked the pickup and looked over at Chloe. "I'll go talk to Blaine. You want to wait here or—"

"I'll go see if Patsy is home," she said. "Be careful."

"You too." They'd both been quiet on the ride out to the ranch. Chloe had been ready and came right out to the truck when he drove up to her house. She looked relieved, as if afraid he was going to renege on picking her up. He wouldn't do that. In the first place, it wouldn't stop her from investigating. He hoped it was safer doing this together. Or maybe it was just giving the killer more prey to go after.

Blaine had looked up when he saw the pickup pull in. Now he stood next to the barn waiting as Justin approached as if he'd been expecting this visit. That was the problem with communities like this. News traveled faster than gale force winds across the prairie. Once Chloe started asking questions, people were going to talk.

"Blaine," he said in greeting. The larger man merely nodded. "I hope you won't take offense, but I need to know if you saw my brother on the day he died."

The man frowned. "Why?"

"Let me rephrase that," Justin said, realizing there was no reason to tiptoe around this. "I need to know if you're the one who beat him up."

PATSY SIMPSON OPENED the door to Chloe's knock and smiled. "I didn't realize we had visitors," she said looking past Chloe to where Justin was talking with Blaine. "Come on in."

Chloe introduced herself. Patsy was four years older and had grown up on a ranch while Chloe had lived in town, so they hadn't known each other. "Justin needed to talk to Blaine, so I drove along."

"Well, come into the kitchen. I was just putting on a pot roast for lunch." She followed the woman into the large farmhouse kitchen. The smell of beef and onions was in the air. "Pull up a stool. I'm almost finished here. Once I pop it into the oven, I'll join you. Coffee?"

She accepted a cup and looked around the homey kitchen as she took a seat at the table. Patsy seemed comfortable and at ease. If she'd heard that anyone had been asking around about Drew Calhoun's death, she didn't show it.

"I thought you might have heard," Chloe said as she watched Patsy put a large cast-iron pot filled with a huge beef roast into the oven and close the door. "Justin and I are trying to find out what was going on with Drew before his death."

The ranch woman seemed to freeze for a moment. When she turned, she smiled. That was, she smiled until Chloe held up the bracelet. All the color drained from her pretty face.

"Justin and I believe that Drew didn't kill himself. I thought you might know who might have wanted him dead."

Patsy stared at the bracelet as it caught the light coming in through the kitchen window. For a moment, she seemed hypnotized. Then she wiped her hands on a dishtowel and with trembling hands poured herself a cup of coffee before joining Chloe at the table.

"When did Drew give you this?"

Patsy hesitated a moment. "In high school when we were dating."

"You kept it all these years?"

The woman shook her head. "I gave it back to him when we broke up."

Chloe studied her for a moment and then took a stab in the dark. "But he gave it back to you."

Patsy nodded. "He was trying to ruin my marriage," she said after taking a sip of the hot coffee. She stared straight ahead as if reliving it for a moment before she turned to face Chloe. "I told him I didn't want the bracelet, that I never wanted to see it again. I thought he took it when he left the ranch that day."

"Your husband found the bracelet?"

The woman looked away for a moment. "I hadn't told him what was going on, that Drew had been out to the ranch when he knew Blaine was in town."

"I would imagine he was angry."

Patsy looked uncomfortable. "Where did you find the bracelet?"

"In his cabin where he died."

Her eyes filled with tears.

"When was the last time you saw the bracelet?" Chloe asked.

The woman straightened as if getting something heavy off her shoulders. "Blaine had it and was going to find Drew." Finally, the truth, Chloe thought. "But I know my husband. He couldn't kill anyone."

"Not even Drew Calhoun, the man who was trying to destroy your marriage?"

BLAINE CHEWED AT his cheek for a moment before looking away. "What are you thinking of doing about it if I was the one who beat up your brother?"

Justin laughed. "I didn't come out here to do a damned thing about it. I'm just trying to figure out a few things."

The rancher nodded as he pushed back his hat to look at him. "Like why he killed himself?" Blaine's gaze softened. "I've struggled with that myself. I was angry with him and had had enough, but if I was why he—"

"You weren't," he quickly assured him. "I don't believe Drew killed himself. I think he was murdered."

The big rancher blinked in surprise. *"Murdered?"*

"That's why I wanted to talk to you. I have a pretty good idea why the two of you argued. But I suspect there was more going on with my brother. I thought you might know what."

Blaine pulled off his weathered Stetson and raked a hand through his hair. "You aren't even going to ask me if I killed him?"

"Would you tell me if you had?"

The rancher chuckled at that before shaking his head. "I told him to leave Patsy alone and he didn't. I kicked his sorry ass and he knew I would do it again. Your brother was his own worst enemy. He was asking for trouble. If you're right, I guess he got it. Truthfully? I felt sorry for him. He'd lost Patsy." He nodded. "She's the best thing that has happened to me so I understand."

ON THE RIDE back to town, Chloe saw the change in Justin. He seemed glad that they'd come out to the Simpson ranch. They shared what they'd learned.

"I don't believe Blaine killed Drew," he said. "He seems like a genuinely nice guy who'd just had enough of Drew. He admitted to kicking his butt though."

"Over the bracelet. Patsy told me that her husband found it and realized Drew had been out to the house. She admitted that he was furious and took the bracelet when he left to go find Drew."

He shook his head. "What was my brother thinking? Or did he care? Blaine actually felt bad, thinking he might have been responsible for why Drew shot himself."

"But you told him that we don't believe that's what happened."

Justin nodded. "Blaine said that something was wrong with my brother. He was always asking for trouble."

"That's interesting because Emily Ferris said Drew didn't feel he deserved being treated so well by your father. He didn't like that he was the favorite son. It made him feel guilty."

Justin shot her a look and then laughed. "He was only trying to get Emily into bed. I don't believe Drew ever felt guilty about anything. But Blaine was right about trouble finding my brother. I can't forget the fear in his eyes that night. Whoever had shot him, Drew looked as if he thought they would be back to finish the job. As it was, another shot wasn't necessary."

Chloe was just about to say that maybe they should take what they knew to the sheriff when she saw the flashing lights behind them in her side mirror. "Were you speeding?" she asked Justin.

"No." He sounded worried as he looked for a place to pull over. They were almost to town. He kept going until they reached the convenience store. Pulling into the back, he parked and waited for whoever was in the patrol SUV to get out.

Chloe groaned when she saw Sheriff's Deputy Kelly Locke climbed out of his patrol SUV and saunter toward them.

"You know him?" Justin said under his breath as he dug out his driver's license and pickup registration.

"Old boyfriend. Bad breakup." She didn't get a chance to say more as Kelly tapped on the window. His gaze was on her as Justin whirred down the driver's side window.

"Out for a little drive?" Kelly said, looking from her to Justin and back.

"There a problem, Deputy?" Justin asked as he handed Kelly his license and registration.

Kelly studied both for a long while before he said, "You might want to slow down."

"Slow down? According to my speedometer I was going under the speed limit." Justin was studying the man. It was clear that he'd noticed that the deputy was more interested in Chloe than him.

"That right?" Kelly asked, the muscle in his jaw worked.

Chloe tensed. She knew better than anyone what this man was like when crossed. How he'd been al-

lowed to become a sheriff's deputy, she had no idea.
But wearing a gun and carrying a badge was definitely something she could see Kelly was enjoying.

Justin shot Chloe a glance, then said, "But I'm
sure your radar gun is more accurate."

The deputy huffed. "You got that right." He handed
back Justin's license and registration. "The two of
you have a nice day."

"What the hell was that?" Justin asked as the deputy drove off.

Chloe let out the breath she'd been holding. "A
long story. Maybe I'll tell you about it some time. I'm
sure he only pulled you over because I was with you."

"If he harasses you—"

"I'll call the sheriff on him."

He shook his head looking worried as the patrol
SUV turned into town and disappeared from view
into the trees that lined the Milk River.

Her cell phone buzzed. "It's my sister Annabelle.
Would you mind dropping me off? Apparently there
is a clothing emergency at my house. The upcom-
ing weddings have them both a little frantic. I'll see
you later?"

Justin nodded. "There's something I need to take
care of, as well. But promise me, no investigating
without me. Deal?"

"Deal." He dropped her off at the house, and as
she started up the walk she noticed a patrol SUV
parked at the end of the street. She couldn't tell who

was behind the wheel at this distance, but she had no doubt. She started to pull out her phone, planning to call the sheriff, when the driver pulled away.

Chapter Fourteen

Justin watched his speed—and his rearview mirror—as he left town. The run-in with the law had him worried. Apparently Deputy Locke had some unfinished business with Chloe given the way the man had been looking at her after he'd pulled them over. Justin definitely wanted to hear about what had happened between them. If Chloe was right about the deputy pulling them over just because she was in the pickup, then that was definitely harassment.

As he drove out to the ranch, he called the hospital to check on his father. Stable and resting. Disconnecting, he could feel the clock ticking. Now they knew who had beaten Drew up the day he died. But they still weren't any closer to finding his…killer. Nor did they know why.

With Drew, trouble usually involved a woman. But he was also in financial trouble apparently. Enough that someone would kill him?

He thought of Nici and hoped to hell he was right about her. He had no doubt where the scratches on

Drew had come from. Nici had been on the ranch that night. He'd seen her car leaving the back way. Still he refused to believe that she'd killed Drew. There had been someone else at his cabin that night because of the second vehicle Justin had heard leaving.

Ahead, the ranch house came into view. He drove in, not seeing anyone around. He told himself that he would do this as quickly as possible. But it was something that had been nagging at him since he'd seen the shape the ranch was in.

He still had a key to the front door, but it wasn't necessary. In this part of Montana hardly anyone locked the doors—especially out in the country. He walked in and headed straight for his father's office.

What he wanted to see were the books. Something was wrong. He could feel it. His father had let things slip, which wasn't like him. But Justin also suspected that in his father's emotional state, there was a good chance that he'd been taken advantage of—maybe for years.

He was digging in his father's desk when he heard a sound behind him.

"What are you doing here?" boomed a male voice behind him.

He recognized it at once and turned to find the big cowboy standing behind him in the doorway. His father's ranch manager, Thane Zimmerman, had a scowl on his face, which wasn't unusual.

"Your father know you're back here?" Thane demanded. Justin had never liked Thane and the feeling was mutual. But then Justin doubted Thane liked anyone. He remembered the resentment he'd seen in Thane's expression when he was around Drew. Even Thane had seen that Drew had no interest in running the ranch.

"My father knows I'm back."

"Back, huh? I doubt he knows you're going through his desk," Thane said.

"I want to see the ranch books."

The ranch manager laughed and crossed his arms. "That's not happening."

"Why is that?"

"You leave and don't come back after all this time? Not to mention how your father feels about you. Hell, we all know that you belong in prison for what you did." The man shook his head. "No, I don't think your father would want you even in this house let alone involved in ranch business."

"My father wouldn't? Or *you* wouldn't?" Justin sighed. He'd felt bullied by this man when he was younger, but not anymore. He took a step toward him. Thane dropped his arms to his sides suddenly looking wary.

"If I'm a killer like you think I am, then you might want to tread more carefully around me. I *will* see the books and if I find what I expect to…" He left the rest hanging. From the man's expression, he'd made his point. Thane looked worried. He should be.

"You should leave before I call the sheriff," the

ranch manager said with more bluster than was behind the words.

"I've already contacted my father's attorney. I will find out what's been going on at this ranch and when I do... I'll be back."

CHLOE LOOKED AT one wedding dress after another as her sisters appeared from the extra downstairs bedroom, which had become Wedding Central. Her sisters had had an assortment of wedding dresses overnighted to them.

"How is the investigation going?" TJ asked after changing out of her last wedding dress and joining Chloe on the couch in the living room.

"We're making a little progress."

"And how is Justin?"

She had to smile. "He's fine."

"Fine?"

"Fine. We've been busy," she groaned. "Get this. Deputy Kelly Locke pulled us over on the way into town this morning. He said Justin was speeding but he wasn't even close to going over the speed limit."

"He's harassing you?" TJ said, instantly getting up in arms.

"And when Justin dropped me off earlier? There was a patrol SUV parked down the street. When I pulled out my phone to call the sheriff, it took off. I can't be sure it was Kelly..."

"I don't like this," TJ said. "If he does anything else, promise me you will notify the sheriff."

Chloe nodded, but getting Kelly in trouble with his boss could make things far worse. Maybe if she just ignored him...

Annabelle came out in another wedding dress.

"That's the one," Chloe exclaimed. TJ agreed and the two of them watched their sister dance around in the dress. "I'm so excited for the two of you," she said, reaching over to take TJ's hand. "I'm so glad we decided to spend the holidays together."

"Me too," TJ said. "Otherwise I wouldn't have met Silas."

"And you and Justin T. Calhoun wouldn't be playing detectives together," Annabelle said.

"Yes," TJ agreed. "Chloe, please, be careful. I know how much you love investigating, but this morning I woke up with a bad feeling."

AFTER RETURNING TO TOWN, Justin found his father's attorney's office closed for the lunch hour. He realized he was hungry as he swung into Joe's In-n-Out and ordered a burger, fries and a chocolate milkshake. He saw Nici pull up. He parked out of the way and waited. A few minutes later she climbed into his truck with her lunch.

She pulled her hamburger from the bag. "You're making enemies," Nici said, as if he didn't already have enough as it was.

He'd waited for her. He opened his lunch bag and drew out his fries. "Anyone in particular?" he asked as he offered her a fry.

Nici shook her head. "I was at the bar last night. Word is out about you being back in town. Drew's friend was there along with a few of his poker buddies. Your ears must have been burning. Thane Zimmerman was there. He'd been drinking and had a lot to say about you."

"Such as?"

She hesitated. "He and Drew's friend said since everyone knows you killed Drew that maybe they would have to take the law into their own hands if they hoped to get Drew justice."

Justin had lost some of his appetite, but he took a bite of his burger as he watched Nici devour hers. "So have you thought any more about what we talked about?"

She swallowed a bite before she said, "Me going to college? Don't you think I'm a little old for that?"

"No. I think you'll actually enjoy it. If you can't afford it—"

"I have some money. I checked and I think there are some grants and scholarships I might be able to get."

He smiled, feeling better, and ate more of his lunch. "Any idea what you'd like to major in?"

"I'm giving it some thought." She shook her head. "Are you just trying to get rid of me?"

"You know better than that. You're my best friend."

She actually seemed to blush as she reached for one of his fries. "Seriously, I'd watch out for Zimmerman."

Justin chuckled. "As a matter of fact, we just had a talk before lunch. There is nothing to worry about."

Nici scoffed at that. "Any closer to finding out who might have shot Drew?"

"Not really. But Chloe and I are definitely making a lot of people nervous." Including his best friend, he thought as Nici looked away.

"CAN I BORROW your car again?" Chloe asked her sister Annabelle that afternoon. Both sisters were waiting for the men in their lives to pick them up for their dates.

"Are you sure you don't want to come along?" TJ said. "I'm sure Silas wouldn't mind. We have the rest of our lives to be together."

She shook her head adamantly. "Absolutely not. You two have a wonderful time. I'll be fine." Chloe could see that TJ was worried about where she planned to go in the car. "I'm driving out to Sleeping Buffalo. I haven't been there in years and the thought of just soaking in the hot pool out there sounds like just what I need for a cold winter afternoon."

Both sisters seemed to relax. She wasn't about to mention that she had an ulterior motive. Annabelle had mentioned earlier during the wedding dress fashion show that Chloe should look into going to work for the local newspaper, the *Milk River Courier*.

"I know it's small and a weekly, but…"

Chloe's ears had perked up when Annabelle had

mentioned the woman who had recently bought the paper.

"Quinn Peterson, do you remember her?" Her sister had asked. "She was working for *The New York Times* before she met her husband and moved back. I think she still freelances for them."

Peterson. "I do remember her. They used to live out by Nelson Reservoir."

"They still do. Built a place next to her folks," Annabelle said.

Chloe had smiled to herself. That meant they lived just down the road from the Sleeping Buffalo. She was so glad that she'd brought her swimming suit. Quinn Peterson was older and had been an inspiration for Chloe. Quinn had worked on the school paper before going into journalism. Also she was a born reporter with a nose for news. She might be exactly the person Chloe needed to talk to.

She thought about her promise to Justin. But she wasn't really investigating and not by herself. Just two newspaper people visiting in the hot pool.

After her sisters left, she called Quinn. They talked for a while before Chloe asked her if she'd like to meet her at the pool.

Justin had found the Gone to Lunch sign down on the attorney's office when he returned from his lunch with Nici. But another sign had been up. This one said the lawyer was in court until four. With time to kill, Justin had driven up into the Little Rockies.

Some of his happiest memories had been camping up there the few times he'd been able to get away from the ranch.

His best friend back then had been Billy Curtis. Billy had lived in town. His father had worked for the city maintenance department. But Billy was gone now. He'd enlisted after high school and had been killed in Iraq.

Justin had some ranch friends, but none he'd kept in touch with. Not that he was in the mood for company. He parked at the campground outside of Zortman and got out. Just the smell of the pines brought back those good memories. He needed them right now.

He drove up to a spot and got out to walk along the snowmobile tracks that led up into the rocky outcroppings until he had a view of the entire valley below him. He'd missed Montana. He'd especially missed this area. But could he stay? Not if he didn't find out the truth about Drew's death.

Justin checked his watch. He needed to get back to town. Climbing back down the mountain, he saw a few deer below him. They watched him warily before trotting off.

He thought of Chloe and wished she'd been there to see them. She would have liked that. He tried her number. It went straight to voice mail. He just hoped she wasn't taking any chances, but she'd promised not to do anything without him. Still, he worried because he'd gotten to know her better.

If she got a lead and couldn't wait for him, she would follow it, sure as hell. Even if it led her straight into trouble.

BACK IN TOWN, Justin drove to the lawyer's office. It was almost four thirty and as he pushed open the main door, he saw that Harry Johnston was in his back office packing up his briefcase to go home. When he looked up, Harry's immediate expression was a frown as he said, "I was just closing up." Then he seemed to recognize Justin and broke into a wide smile.

Leaving what he was doing, the attorney reached out his hand to shake Justin's. The man had a firm grip and an easygoing manner, but Justin knew the reason his father had hired him was because Harry Johnston was tough as nails.

"I saw that you'd called," the older man said, waving him into his office and closing the door. "I heard about your father. I'm so sorry. How is he doing?"

"Last time I spoke with the doctor, he was stable."

Harry waved him into a chair and took his behind the desk. "Bert's strong. He can beat this."

Justin wished he believed that. "Drew's death hit him hard." The attorney nodded. "This cloud over my head hasn't helped. I'm trying to sort that out."

"No, the questions around your brother's death haven't helped," Harry agreed. "So what can I do to help?"

"It's about the ranch. I was shocked to realize that

my father has lost his interest in it apparently," Justin said. "I'm worried and quite frankly, I don't trust Thane Zimmerman, never have."

The attorney nodded. "Your father saw something in him few others have."

"I want to see the ranch books. Zimmerman is determined to keep them from me. I know legally I might not be able to—"

"There's no reason you can't see the books. Ray Underwood is your father's accountant. I'll give him a call and tell him to give you whatever you need."

"Wait," Justin said. "I thought—"

"Son, your name is on that ranch—just like your brother's was. Your father never changed that."

He sat for a moment in shock. He'd been expecting a fight. Relief washed over him. He'd never known that his father planned to leave both sons the ranch. All his life his father had talked about Drew getting the ranch. Or at least running it.

"Thank you."

Harry rose and shook his hand again. "I'm glad you're home and it's good that you're sorting things out. You let me know if I can help you further. I'll give Ray a call right away."

CHLOE LOVED SLEEPING BUFFALO. The pools had been redone over the last few years making the natural hot springs beautiful. Chloe was lounging in the hottest pool when Quinn arrived. She was just as Chloe remembered her, wild curly red hair and violet eyes. But it was her smile that lit up rooms and no doubt, helped her as a journalist.

As Quinn slipped into the pool across from her, she said, "Okay, what is this really about?"

Chloe laughed. "I suspect you already know."

"Drew Calhoun's death. You investigating it for that paper you're working for in California?"

She shook her head. "I got caught up in the layoffs. I'm doing it because I'm disturbed by what I've found out about his death. I believe he was murdered."

Quinn raised a brow, but she didn't look all that surprised. "I chased the story for a little while, but being the local paper..."

Chloe understood too well. "You were closer to Drew's age than me. What can you tell me?"

Quinn laughed and lay back in the water for a moment. Steam rose from the pool. They had it to themselves this evening since everyone else was probably just getting home from work and thinking about dinner.

"Drew. A lot of people didn't like him."

"Tell me something I don't know," Chloe said with a laugh. "Who would want him dead enough to pull the trigger?"

Quinn sighed. "I did hear something, but I wasn't able to verify it. The mine at Zortman? There was a rumor it might open again."

Chloe felt her heart drop. That rumor had been

going around as long as she could remember. "Even if it's true, what could that have to do with Drew's death?"

"Supposedly there was a group of secret investors who were putting the deal together. Drew Calhoun was rumored to be one of them." Quinn shrugged. "I asked him about it before he died. He denied it, but he got more upset than I thought he should have. He wanted to know who'd told me. It seemed a little strange. But I couldn't find anyone else who knew anything about it."

Chloe thought about that for a long moment but came up with no reason why someone would kill over it. Even if he was one of the secret investors. A lot of people would have loved to see the mine open again because of jobs. The mine had provided some of the best-paying jobs around. When it pulled out, a lot of people thought the town of Whitehorse would die.

"I heard the gold had run out up there," she said to Quinn.

"There's not just gold and apparently there are new methods of getting the ore out. But it's expensive."

"Hmm, doesn't sound like anything that would get Drew killed."

"There was a little more to it, as it turned out. The group was racing against the clock to make a deal before a pending EPA study. They wouldn't have had to do a lot of reclamation if they beat the deadline. So if one of the investors dropped out at the last minute, they would have lost their chance. I did some research on the mine. Those secret investors could have made a lot of money. But once the EPA stepped in, it became too expensive with the reclamation. I dropped my inquiries when I found out that Drew didn't have the money to invest in the deal."

"But his father would have," Chloe said.

"If Drew had been able to get his hands on the ranch, you mean."

"Maybe he thought he could and when he couldn't..." Quinn shrugged.

"The other investors would have been furious. Maybe enough to kill him."

HARRY WAS GOOD to his word. Justin got the call on his way out to the Rogers Ranch. He swung around and went back into Whitehorse. Ray Underwood lived on the east end of town near the new hospital. This was the area that had seen what little growth there had been in Whitehorse.

The house was a nice newer split-level with a two-car garage. Ray answered the bell and motioned Justin down the stairs to his home office. The man was slightly built and only a little younger than Justin's father, so in his late fifties.

"I hope I'm not interrupting your dinner," Justin told him. When he'd come in, he'd caught the scent of meat loaf if he had to guess.

"Not a problem. Harry said you needed these right away so I pulled them out for you and made copies." He handed Justin a thick stack of papers. "These are the taxes from the past five years along with the most recent quarterlies. I also included the five years before that."

He couldn't help but smile. The man was so efficient. "Thank you so much."

"My pleasure. I've enjoyed working with your father for years."

A thought struck him. "Is that who you've been working with recently, my father? Or Thane Zimmerman?" He saw at once that he'd been right.

"Your father hasn't been…well."

"I'm going to take a wild guess. The ranch isn't doing as well as it used to."

Ray hesitated but only a moment. "It's all in those papers, but…no." The accountant looked away. "But you will see that the trouble began before that."

Justin didn't need to ask. Nor did he want to put the man on the spot. Something wasn't right and Ray knew it.

AFTER ENJOYING THE POOLS, Chloe left Sleeping Buffalo feeling more relaxed than she'd been for a while. The hot spring water had been so refreshing. She told herself she should take more advantage of the pools. Until she left after the New Year to look for a new job, she reminded herself.

She hadn't gone far when snow began to fall. The

storm that had been forecast blew in with a fury. She slowed down. It wasn't like she was in a hurry. She wondered what Justin was up to tonight. Earlier, he'd sent her a text saying he hoped she had a good night. She had and only felt a little guilty for her "swim." Yes, she had kind of been investigating, but it had been perfectly safe.

Chloe was on the edge of town when she saw flashing lights come on behind her. She hadn't seen any other traffic for some time. She hurriedly looked down to see how fast she was going. The speed limit. Her gaze shot to the rearview mirror as she debated what to do. She couldn't tell if it was a sheriff's deputy patrol SUV or a Montana Highway Patrol.

Chloe was thinking about earlier when Kelly had pulled Justin over to harass him. He wouldn't do that again, would he? The patrol SUV was right behind her, the lights blinding her. She braked and pulled over next to the plowed snowbank on the edge of the highway.

Once stopped, she reached over to open the glove compartment to look for the car registration. But she also pulled out her phone. In the side mirror, she saw the officer get out of his patrol SUV. She froze and swore, then grabbed her phone and hit Record.

Sheriff's Deputy Kelly Locke moved to the driver's side as she put down her window, making sure that her phone video recorded whatever was about to go down. She would have proof when she went to the sheriff. That was the only thing that kept her calm as he leaned down to look into her car at her.

"What did I do wrong, officer?" she asked.

"What have you done right?" He sounded angry.

She looked straight head at the lights of White-horse and realized even recording this she was taking a risk. She'd pulled over in an isolated area. Worse, there was no traffic tonight. There was no one to help her. Her pulse kicked up with apprehension.

"I wasn't speeding," she said. "So what is the problem?"

Kelly looked away for a moment as if checking for traffic. Chloe checked her rearview mirror and saw headlights behind her in the distance.

When the deputy glanced at her again, she saw his jaw tighten. "I think you'd better get out of the car after this vehicle goes past."

Her heart rate leaped with alarm. No way was she getting out let alone going anywhere with this man. She reached for her phone and hit Send before she began video recording again.

"What are you doing?" he demanded.

"I just emailed a video recording of this to my sister." The vehicle that had been behind them whizzed past. "You don't mind if I record this conversation, do you, Deputy Locke? I want it on the record why you pulled me over. And why you're asking me to get out of my car."

His face was a mask of fury. "You were speeding."

"Do you have that documented, Deputy Locke? Because when you pulled me over I looked down at my speedometer right away and I wasn't going near the speed limit."

He looked like he might explode. "I'm going to just give you a warning this time. You were going too fast for the conditions tonight. Just be careful." She could see him grinding his teeth. "Be very careful." With that he turned and started to walk away. She put her phone down with trembling fingers as she watched him in her side mirror.

Kelly was almost past the rear of the car when she saw him pull out his baton and turn to look at her as if he was thinking about coming back. Her mind screamed "No!" Not taking her eyes off him, she fumbled for the button for her side window. Her pulse pounded but before she could get her window up—

She jumped at the sound of glass shattering. Kelly was standing at the rear of the car looking right at her.

"You'd better have someone fix that broken taillight. I'd hate to have to pull you over again. Next time, you won't get off so easily," he said.

Trembling with fear and relief, she got her side window up and made sure her doors were locked as he climbed behind the wheel of the patrol SUV. She waited until he pulled out and drove slowly past her toward town before she felt she could breathe normally again.

He'd broken the taillight on Annabelle's car! Unfortunately, she hadn't gotten that on the recording she'd made.

Chapter Fifteen

It didn't take Justin long to see the pattern. But what threw him was when it had started. He suspected with his father not paying attention, Thane was helping himself to some of the ranch profits. That much at least was clear.

But his father had been in charge of the ranch and aware of things before Drew's death. The losses began two years before then.

Justin stared at the paperwork until his head hurt. He finally had to put it away for the night. Two things were clear. Someone had been taking money out of the ranch fund two years before Drew died—and continued after his death.

It made no sense. His father would have noticed— at least before Drew's death. Bert Calhoun was a businessman first and a rancher second. Justin knew firsthand how careful he'd been about money. His father could have told you how much the ranch made in a year right down to the cents.

So what had happened? He suspected it had been Drew. He knew his father had been grooming him to take over the ranch. All he could think was during those two years, his father had given Drew more authority—and his brother had taken advantage of it. That would explain why their father had cut Drew off before his death.

He couldn't believe it. But it appeared Drew had been stealing from the ranch company. He was sure Drew hadn't seen it that way. He probably thought it was his money, his birthright, so why not spend some of it while he was young.

But it hadn't been extra spending money. Justin realized it was thousands of dollars. What had his brother done with that money? Gambled it all away? Or had he hung on to it? In that case, where was it?

He made a mental note to check at the bank tomorrow and headed for bed. But he knew he wasn't going to be able to sleep. His mind was racing. Money had continued to disappear *after* Drew's death. Not as much, but there was only one person who could have been taking it.

Thane Zimmerman. It was the only explanation unless his father had taken it from the ranch profits for some reason.

He realized he was going to have to talk to his father about this. It was a conversation he wasn't looking forward to, fearing it might bring on another health crisis that could be lethal.

"YOU NEED TO take this recording to the sheriff," TJ said the next morning at breakfast. The three of them were sitting about the table. Annabelle had made blueberry coffee cake. Chloe had awakened to the scent of it and told herself she couldn't keep eating like this as she got dressed and rushed down for a piece while it was still warm.

She'd told her sisters about what happened when she'd gotten home. They'd been horrified and had wanted her to call the sheriff right then. "If I do, it could only make it worse. What if she fires him? Or suspends him? He'll still be out there and he'd be even more vindictive."

"But he won't be wearing a gun or carrying a badge," TJ pointed out. "And he won't be pulling you over for no reason."

"You should get a restraining order," Annabelle said and took a sip of her coffee.

TJ was shaking her head. "They're worthless if the person thinks he is above the law and Kelly Locke is a perfect example of that. You have to take this to the sheriff and tell her what happened, Chloe. This man needs to be stopped."

Last night, she'd lain in bed debating what to do. There was no doubt that he was dangerous.

"I don't understand why he is doing any of this now," TJ said.

"Because I broke up with him in high school. You wouldn't believe the terrible things he did back then to get back at me. Believe me that was plenty of retribution."

"I know he put you through hell," TJ said. "You didn't have to say anything," she added seeing Chloe's surprise. "I heard about it at school. I didn't know how to help you back then. I was afraid of standing up to him for fear he would make it harder on you. Also that he'd start on me. But I'm not fifteen anymore."

Chloe knew her sister was right. "Okay, I'll stop by and see the sheriff. I just hope I don't run into him, although if he thought I had everything on the recording including him breaking the taillight on the car, he might back off."

Her sisters were shaking their heads.

She feared they were right. "Talk about carrying a grudge."

"It's pretty classic," TJ said, who studied character traits in criminals. "He had it all in high school— popular, a star athlete, he was somebody. I'm sure he felt he was doing any girl he dated a favor. Then you break up with him and send him into a tailspin. Not only that, word got around school. He's had to live with that rejection for years. Just the sight of you or even his knowing you're in town, probably brings back that humiliation as if it was yesterday."

Chloe finished her coffee, considered another piece of the blueberry coffee cake, and talked herself out of it. "I'm going to get this over with."

"Do you want us to come with you?" Annabelle asked.

"No, you two have weddings to plan. It's only

days until the big event," Chloe said. "I'll be fine. I've run up against angry people who wanted to blame my reporting of what they did, instead of accepting responsibility for their misdeed. But I've never had anyone hate me like this. I have to admit, he scares me. Last night on that deserted highway with him…" She shuddered.

"This might not stop him," TJ said. "But whatever the sheriff does about it, he'll know he's being watched."

"So he'll be more careful next time," Chloe said.

TJ nodded. "Just don't let him get you alone."

BERT CALHOUN WAS sitting up in bed when his son tapped at the hospital room door. He saw that Justin was surprised to see him looking so much better. He knew he'd come close to dying a couple of times. But they'd brought him back and now more than ever he was determined to live.

He motioned his son into the room and pointed to the chair next to his bed where Justin had been sitting the other day. Bert felt bad that he hadn't acknowledged his presence that day. When he'd come close to death, he'd sworn he'd seen Mary. She'd given him a good tongue-lashing. Dream or not, it had made him feel small and ashamed.

Justin sat down on the chair next to his bed, Stetson dangling from his fingers. "How are you feeling?"

His voice came out on a hoarse whisper. "Better."

"I can see that. They said you had another heart attack."

Bert nodded. "I thought I saw your mother. She's worried about you." He saw that Justin looked worried that his father had lost his marbles. "I'm fine so you can quit looking at me like that."

"I see they've moved you out of ICU," Justin said. "That's good."

"You don't have to treat me like I'm made of glass," he snapped and quickly regretted it. "I'm sorry about the other day."

Justin nodded. "So am I."

He noticed that his son had brought in a stack of papers. "What's that?"

"Tax information on the ranch for the past seven years, but I won't ask you about it if it's going to upset you," his son said, adding the last part quickly.

Bert took a few breaths. He could feel himself starting to get worked up. He wanted to demand what Justin thought he was doing butting into ranch business. But he remembered that Justin's name was on the ranch and Harry would have helped him with anything his son asked.

"So you know," he finally said and reached for the cup of water next to his bed. He managed to knock it over.

Justin was on his feet, catching the cup before very much spilled. "You need a drink?"

He chuckled. He could use a strong one right now,

but he merely nodded. Justin held it up so he could take a sip from the straw. "I hate being this helpless."

"I know." Justin sat back down. "If you don't want to tell me…"

Bert didn't want to tell anyone. Just the thought made him angry. But he took a few more deep breaths as the doctor had told him he needed to start doing. It went against his nature, but if he didn't want to end up in a box six feet under, he had little choice but to make some changes.

"It was Drew, but I suspect you've already figured that out," he said, hating to admit that his oldest son had stolen from him, from the legacy that Bert had always thought would someday be his. Of course, Drew had at first denied what he'd done and then argued that it was his money so what was the big deal.

"What did he use the money for?" Justin asked.

"Who knows? Gambling, women or some get-rich scheme. I let it go too long, I'm ashamed to say." He closed his eyes. He'd let a lot of things go too long.

"I think he might have owed someone a lot of money and when he couldn't pay, they came after him for it," Justin said.

Bert realized what he was getting at. "You still think someone…" He swallowed and breathed for a moment. He didn't even want to say the words *killed Drew*. "He wanted me to step down and let him take over the ranch. He wasn't ready, no matter what he said. Truth is, I knew I couldn't trust him."

"Did he seem desperate for money?"

Bert let out a huff. "He was always desperate for money. He had some big deal he was involved in. He actually wanted me to give him five hundred thousand dollars so he could invest it in some fly-by-night operation with some of his buddies."

"Did he tell you what it was?" Justin asked.

He shook his head. "I didn't care. I told him I couldn't come up with that much money. He demanded that I cosign a loan, using the ranch as collateral. You can imagine how well that went over. I'd had it with him. We argued." He hated to think about it since it was the last time he saw his oldest son alive. "He was so angry, so hateful." He closed his eyes, the pain too much for him. He'd been so disappointed in Drew because by then, he'd known that his son had been stealing from the ranch. They hadn't spoken after that. He opened his eyes. "Wait, did you say the past *seven* years money was taken out?"

"You've had a lot on your mind," Justin said.

"Don't you be making excuses for me. If money has still been going out..." Bert tried to sit up.

"I didn't come here to upset you, but yes. Not as much as those two years previous to Drew's death, but someone is still helping himself."

"Zimmerman," he said and leaned back and closed his eyes as he swore under his breath. He hadn't been paying attention because of Drew's death and he was getting old. That made him all the more angry that his ranch manager would take advantage of him like that.

"I'll take care of it," Justin said, getting to his feet. "That is, if it's all right with you."

Bert opened his eyes. He smiled and nodded. "I'd like to fire the son of a B myself but the doctor said I need to start working on my temper."

"You get some rest and don't worry about anything," Justin said as he rose to leave.

"Son? I'm sorry." He started to say more, but his son stopped him.

"We're both sorry, but I'm home now. I'll help any way I can. You'll be on your feet soon."

Bert nodded, tears in his eyes. "I'm glad you're home."

JUSTIN DROVE OUT to the ranch. He suspected that what he had to say to Thane Zimmerman would not come as a surprise. The moment the ranch manager had caught him in Bert's desk, he would have known he was in trouble. Once Justin told him he would be talking to the family lawyer, Thane wasn't stupid enough to think he was going to get away with what he'd been doing.

As he pulled up in front of the large cabin where Thane lived on the ranch, he saw that the back of the man's pickup was already loaded. He got out and walked toward the cabin. He knew what he wanted to do and had he been younger, he just might have done it.

But since returning home, Justin knew he had to be what his father needed right now. And that wasn't his son getting into a fistfight with their former ranch manager just because he was angry and would have loved nothing bettter. Not to mention the fact that he knew Thane well enough to know that he would have him thrown in jail for assault and probably bring a lawsuit against him.

He knocked at the door. A harried Thane answered. Surprise registered on his face but only for a moment. He'd probably thought he could get away before Justin even had copies of the ranch accounts. He'd been wrong and it showed in his expression.

"I guess I don't have to tell you that you're fired," Justin said, glancing past him to where Thane had been filling more boxes.

"You can't fire me. I quit," the man said belligerently.

"Just don't take anything that isn't yours," he said. "Once my father is out of the hospital, he'll decide if he wants to sue you for the money you stole from the ranch. I wouldn't count on an employment recommendation."

"You think you're so damned smart, don't you?" Thane blustered. "It wouldn't take much to knock you down to size. If I were you—"

"You're not me. You never will be. And keep trying to stir up trouble down at the bar in town and I will see that you're locked behind bars until the accountant can come up with the exact amount you stole from this ranch," Justin said.

With that he turned and walked away, half expecting Thane to come after him, half hoping he would. The man made him forget about being a responsible adult right then.

But maybe Thane wasn't as stupid as he looked, Justin thought. Because all the man did was mumble obscenities under his breath and slam the door.

CHLOE COULDN'T HELP being nervous as she entered the sheriff's department building. The last person she wanted to run into was Deputy Kelly Locke.

She was sent straight back to Sheriff McCall Crawford's office. She stepped in and closed the door behind her, making the sheriff lift an eyebrow in question.

"Is this about your private investigation?" McCall asked.

Chloe shook her head. "This is about another matter. I don't know if you're aware of this, but I dated one of your deputies in high school. It ended badly. I broke it off and he became vindictive, doing his best to ruin my senior year. But I survived it and put it behind me. Unfortunately, it seems he didn't."

She pulled out her phone and handed it across the desk to the sheriff. "This wasn't the first time he's been threatening, but last night he pulled me over. I was scared so I recorded it." She let the sheriff watch it before she said. "Unfortunately, I turned off the recording after that. Deputy Kelly Locke took out his baton as he walked back toward his patrol SUV and broke the taillight on my sister's car, then said,

'You'd better have someone fix that broken taillight. I'd hate to have to pull you over again. Next time, you won't get off so easily.'"

The sheriff said nothing as she watched it a second time. "Is your taillight still busted?"

Chloe nodded. "I'll try to get it fixed for my sister as soon as I can get it in the shop, but with the holidays..."

The sheriff nodded. "I'll take care of the repair. You can leave the car here. But if you have any further problems with him, you call me right away."

"Thank you." She turned to leave but stopped when the sheriff called her name and asked if she needed a ride. Chloe shook her head no.

Sheriff Crawford added, "Chloe, be careful. I still believe that Drew Calhoun's death was an accident but sometimes just asking questions can be dangerous."

As she left, Justin called. She took the call outside in the cold rather than chance seeing Kelly. Last night's snow was piled high all over town.

"Where are you?" She told him. "Don't move. I'll pick you up."

JUSTIN PULLED UP in front of the sheriff's office and Chloe hopped into the passenger side of his pickup. She looked beautiful. The cold clear morning had her cheeks pink and those blue eyes glittering.

"Is everything all right?" he asked glancing toward the sheriff's department.

She waved a hand through the air. "I'll tell you later. First I want to tell you what I found out last night."

He glanced at her sideways. "I thought you weren't going to do anything without me?"

"I just went swimming with the new owner of the local newspaper out at Sleeping Buffalo."

Justin groaned as he pulled away from the curb. He listened as she told him about the rumor concerning the reopening of the mine. "So Drew didn't have the money."

"But what if he'd thought he would be able to get it?" Chloe said. "What if he'd made promises he couldn't keep? Apparently the group had to get the deal done before some EPA study that was scheduled. They wouldn't have had to do the reclamation if they beat the deadline so there was big money to be made. But what if at the last minute Drew reneged and the deal fell through?"

Justin nodded. "You could be onto something. I got hold of the ranch books. My brother had been stealing money for about two years before my father cut him off. I just saw my father this morning. He's out of intensive care. He said Drew was desperate for money for some deal he was involved in and needed five hundred thousand dollars. Apparently my brother thought the deal would make him rich."

Chloe looked at him wide-eyed. "That's a lot of money. That could be the deal. Quinn said the investors stood to make a whole bunch of money. If Drew couldn't raise his part right before the deadline…"

"Who were the other investors?" Justin said. "And how do we find them?"

She seemed to give that some thought. "I know at least one place to start. Monte Decker at the bank."

"MR. DECKER IS on vacation," the teller told Chloe. The bank like the town was small. There was one counter with four tellers. Two offices at the front of the bank and several in the back. In a place where everyone knew each other, the atmosphere was casual. As far as she knew, the bank had never been robbed.

"When will he be back?" Chloe asked.

"I'm not sure. Is there someone else who can help you?"

"No, I'll catch him when he returns." As she started out of the bank, she glanced into Monte's office and noticed something that made her stop cold.

The photo she'd seen on his desk of him and the huge walleye was gone.

"I have a bad feeling that Monte is leaving town," Chloe said as she climbed into Justin's pickup parked outside the bank with the engine running. "Do you know where he lives?"

"I know where he used to live." He shifted the pickup into gear and started out of town. "Unless he's moved, his family had an old place out by Dobson. His parents left him the land. I only know because Drew mentioned a few times how lucky we were that our old man had built something substantial for us to inherit, compared to poor Monte, who had to work at the bank to survive. Drew loved to lord it over Monte."

"And Monte was the one who allegedly lost all the money to your brother before he found out Drew had been cheating at cards."

Justin shook his head. "There was something seriously wrong with my brother. He was always like that. Everything was a competition for him. He had to win. If he was one of those investors, he must have seen it as a way to get out from under the ranch. Taking over Calhoun Cattle Company must have felt like a noose around his neck. But a mining operation where he could sit back and rake in the money without our father involved… That would have felt like his way out."

He slowed on the outskirts of what was left of the rural town. The businesses had shrunk down to schools and one convenience store. The bar had closed recently. Monte Decker's place was down a long dirt road that ended at the Milk River. A gray Suburban was parked in front of the small old two-story house. As they pulled in, Monte came out with two large suitcases. He stopped when he saw them before continuing on to the back of the Suburban.

"Going somewhere?" Justin asked as he and Chloe got out to confront the man.

"Vacation," Monte said. "Not that it is any of your business."

Chloe knew they couldn't stop him from leaving town. "You need to tell us about the group of investors who was going to start mining at Zortman again." She saw by his expression that she'd hit pay dirt and that Justin had seen it, as well.

Monte appeared rattled. His gaze shot to the road into his property as if he expected more company. The sheriff? Or someone else?

"We also know that my brother was one of the investors," Justin said as if he too was sure they were right about all this. "At least he was supposed to have been one of them, right?"

Monte slammed the back of the Suburban. "I don't know what you're talking about," he said, his words lacking even a semblance of truth to them. "I need to get going."

"We know the truth," Justin said. "The sheriff is on the way."

"There was nothing illegal about it."

"Not about the mining deal, but murder..." Justin said.

Monte looked around as if searching for a place to run. When they'd pulled in, they'd blocked his Suburban. He'd have to take out part of the fence around his house to escape. That's if they let him get that far.

"Drew ruined it all for you, didn't he?" Chloe said. "First he cheats you at cards and then he stiffs all of you on the deal of a lifetime." She saw the answer in the man's eyes. For Monte and who knew how many others, it had been a way out of the life they were living into one they'd only dreamed possible.

"How much money were you putting up?" Chloe asked. "Were you using your money or were you getting it from the bank?" For a moment, she didn't think he was going to answer.

"It was my money," he snapped indignantly. "Two hundred thousand, but it only bought me a minor share."

"But you stood to make a lot of money," Justin said.

"Nothing like the rest of them. It was a legit, good business deal."

"Then Drew screwed up everything," Justin said.

Monte swore. He looked caught, a man no longer believing he was going to get away. "We knew that we had to have all the money together before we could make the offer. We had to move fast. It was all about timing. We thought everyone understood that." He looked like he might cry. "Like I said, I was only a minor player."

"So did they make you kill him?" Justin asked.

"No!" Panic filled the man's face. "You have it all wrong." He looked down the road as if expecting to see a vehicle tearing toward them. Who was he expecting? "It wasn't me!"

"I believe you," Chloe said, almost feeling sorry for him. "But you know who did."

"And I'm guessing that you know it's all over," Justin said. "The one who pulled the trigger? You know you can't trust him. Now that the sheriff knows, he'll turn on you and when he does—"

Monte took a step backward, holding up his hands as if to ward off their words. "I had nothing to do with killing Drew. I swear I tried to stop it. I—"

Chloe didn't hear the rifle shot until after she heard the thump of the bullet when it entered Monte's body. She froze, too shocked to move as Monte grabbed his chest.

But Justin must have known immediately what was happening and where the shot had come from. He grabbed her and pulled her behind the Suburban as another bullet hit its mark with another sicking thud. She heard Monte say something. Two more bullets struck the Suburban they were crouched behind, making a pinging sound. Justin had his arm around her, shielding her as he punched in 911 on his phone.

Then, everything went deathly still.

Chapter Sixteen

"The gunshots appeared to be coming from up there," Justin said, pointing to the foothills opposite the road from Monte Decker's house. The sheriff nodded and wrote something in her notebook as Chloe stood off to the side, hugging herself to try to get some warmth back into her body. She couldn't quit shivering.

Justin had taken off his coat and put it around her. They'd sat in his pickup until the sheriff had arrived along with the coroner. Photographs were taken, the area searched and taped off. The coroner's van had left with Monte in a black body bag.

McCall had said that Chloe could remain in the pickup, but she'd felt too closed in. She needed the fresh air even if it was freezing cold. Nearby a deputy was digging bullets out of the side of Monte's Suburban. She tried not to think about the bullets that would have to be dug out of Monte's body during his autopsy.

"Are you all right?" the sheriff asked. Justin was talking to another lawman.

McCall had already taken her statement. "You need to get in out of the cold."

She nodded, but didn't move.

"I already asked you this, but I thought now that you've had time to think about it…" The sheriff was studying her. "Any idea who else might have been part of these investors you told me about?"

Chloe shook her head. They hadn't even been sure the rumor was true until they talked to Monte. He'd been so terrified they'd known they were on the right track. "Maybe one of the others who played poker with Drew." That was her best guess. Nor did she know how many men had been involved. Not many, she thought. Otherwise it would have been harder to keep a secret. "Someone with more than two hundred thousand dollars to invest."

"So you don't know how much Drew's part was?" the sheriff asked.

Chloe was sure that Justin had already told her. "Justin said his father mentioned five hundred thousand dollars. That's how much he wanted to borrow against the ranch for an investment. Bert Calhoun didn't know what investment."

McCall nodded and closed her notebook. "By the way, Deputy Kelly Locke has been suspended of his duties without pay for two weeks."

Was that supposed to make her happy?

"If you have any more problems…"

"You'll be the first to know," Chloe said, thinking Kelly was the least of her problems right now."

"Also I'd advise you to stay out of this investigation since it now involves a homicide," the sheriff said. "If I have any more questions…"

"You know where to find me," she said and looked to where Justin had finished talking to the deputy. She excused herself and walked over to him. He put his arm around her and pulled her close, pressing a kiss into her hair.

"I'm so sorry I got you into this," he whispered.

She pulled back to look into his handsome face. "I'm the one who's sorry."

"I need to take you to your house. Why don't you call and make sure your sisters are there? I'm not leaving you alone and I have a couple of things I have to take care of."

She worried what that might be, but maybe it had something to do with his father and the ranch. She was sure that the sheriff had warned him too about getting involved in her investigation.

He looked into her eyes. "You'll be all right?"

Chloe nodded. She was shaken. It wasn't every day that someone tried to kill her or that she saw a man gunned down in front of her. Not that she thought Monte Decker would still be alive if she and Justin hadn't driven out to talk to him. Whoever had killed Drew must have known that Monte was a weak link in the cover-up. Monte would have never gotten to leave. Chloe and Justin had just been in the wrong place at the wrong time.

Fortunately, Monte hadn't been killed before they talked to him. Otherwise they wouldn't have had verification that their theory had been right. Drew was involved with the secret group who'd planned to get mining approval before the EPA got involved.

First Drew. Now Monte. Who'd killed them? And what was that person going to do now? Whoever the killer was, he couldn't know how much Monte had told them before he'd fired the fatal shots.

JUSTIN WAITED UNTIL she was safely in the house, making sure that her sisters were both home, before he left. He had two quick stops to make before he went to see his father. He called Nici's house and found out she was doing community service down at the senior center.

"I am so glad to see you," she said. "Get me out of here."

"Is your time up?" he asked.

"Close enough." She called back to one of the managers and asked if she could leave. The woman said she could and that they would see her the next day and not to be late again.

Nici mugged a face as they left. "How did you know I needed to see a friendly face?"

"Maybe not so friendly," Justin said as they climbed into this pickup. "Something's happened. Monte Decker was killed this afternoon at his place."

"One of Drew's poker-playing friends," Nici said.

"It's all going to come out, everything," he said. "I have to tell the sheriff the truth about that night. Nici—"

"I told you I didn't kill Drew."

"But you were there," Justin said, meeting her gaze. "If you saw Drew's killer…"

She shook her head and looked away.

He cursed under his breath. "Damn it, Nici, this is getting even more dangerous. Why, if you saw him, won't you tell me?"

She opened the passenger side door and started to climb out.

He grabbed her arm. "I know you're scared. You should be. If there is any chance that the killer knows you were out there that night… You've kept your mouth shut, but that person isn't going to take the chance that you won't talk now."

"I told you. I didn't kill Drew. I didn't see anything." She jerked her arm free and got out, standing in the open doorway for a moment as she looked back at him.

"I have to tell the sheriff, Nici. I should have that night."

She nodded and smiled. "Thanks for trying to protect me. You've been a good friend." She slammed the door and took off walking, her hands deep in the pockets of her coat.

Justin swore as he watched her walk away before he drove down to the sheriff's office. After he made his way into the station, McCall motioned him into a chair.

"This won't take long," he said, turning his Stetson in his fingers. "The night my brother was killed, Nici, Nicole Kent, was at the ranch. I saw her drive away just moments after I heard the shots. She'd parked just over the hill. I recognized her rig leaving."

"Why couldn't you have told me this years ago?" the sheriff demanded.

"Because she'd already been in trouble with the law and she's a friend. Also, I don't believe she killed him. But I'm afraid she saw the killer."

McCall groaned. "And there's a reason she too hasn't come forward?"

"No doubt. Unfortunately, I don't know what it is, but I'm worried about her given what's happened and what we now know." He got to his feet. "She knows I planned to tell you."

The sheriff nodded. "You realize your warning her has given her a head start if she's on the run now."

"I'm sorry about that," he said. "But she's a friend and she needs a friend right now—maybe more than ever."

"I HAD A bad feeling that this was going to be dangerous," TJ said as the three sisters congregated in the kitchen. Annabelle made coffee while Chloe told them what had happened. She served the coffee with her latest batch of sugar cookies.

"Monte knew who killed Drew," Chloe said. "If we'd had just a few more minutes…"

"Then the killer doesn't know that Monte didn't spill his guts to you," Annabelle said and looked at TJ. "Doesn't this mean he'll come after Chloe?"

"This is not one of my books," her sister snapped. "But that is certainly a possibility. What does Justin think?"

Chloe shrugged. "After we gave our statements to the sheriff, he brought me home. We didn't talk much about it." The truth was, she'd seen that Justin had something on his mind. Why did she suspect he knew something more than he was telling her and had been from the get-go?

"Well, I hope this is the end of your investigation," TJ said.

"The sheriff warned me to cease and desist, but it wasn't necessary. If you'd been there and heard… It was horrible. If Justin hadn't pulled me behind Monte's vehicle when he did…" Chloe cupped her hands around her mug of coffee needing the warmth. She still felt chilled.

"So you have no idea who the other investors were?" TJ asked.

She shook her head. "Whoever they are, they had to have gotten their hands on a sizeable amount of money to be part of the plan. Monte said he put two hundred thousand into the pot and he was a minor in-

vestor. Justin's father told him that Drew had needed
five hundred thousand."

"So it could have been several million if there had
been five or six investors," TJ said.

Annabelle raised an eyebrow. "Who has that kind
of cash?"

TJ met Chloe's gaze. "Follow the money," they
said in unison.

She was surprised when her phone rang and it
was Justin.

"I'm on my way to the hospital to see my father.
Would you like to go with me?"

"Really?"

"I'd love the company and truthfully, a pretty
young woman might be exactly what he needs right
now," Justin said.

"I'd love to meet him."

"I'll be over shortly," he said. "I have one more
thing I need to do."

HE COULD FEEL everything closing in on him, but
he tried to remain calm. He pictured himself holding the rifle lying on the top of the hill overlooking
Monte Decker's ranch. Finger on the trigger. Breath
in, breath out. He'd known he had to hit his mark
the first time or he might not get a second chance.

An avid hunter, he'd been shooting since he was
nine. He'd spent hours plinking tin cans off the fence
at the ranch. That had been child's play.

He still practiced because when he hunted, he

prided himself on a clean kill. He couldn't bear to see an animal suffer.

Monte had been lucky. The first shot alone should have killed him.

But he hadn't been able to take the chance that it hadn't, so he'd fired again and watched him drop. Through the scope, he saw that Monte wasn't moving. He wouldn't be moving again. The damned fool had planned to run. He'd tried to talk him out of it.

I have everything under control, he'd told the banker. *Run and it will only make you look guilty.*

He'd known just listening to how nervous and upset Monte had been that he would have to take care of him. Monte would talk. He wouldn't be able to help himself. He'd get scared and blab.

He didn't consider himself a killer. Taking out Monte had been like killing a rabid dog. Even if you loved the dog, you had to put it down. That's how he felt about Monte. Not that he'd loved him. But he'd liked him well enough.

Unfortunately, Justin Calhoun and that nosy reporter had shown up too quickly. He had no way of knowing how much Monte had told them before he died—and that was now a problem that would also have to be dealt with. He'd know soon enough—if the sheriff showed up at his door. Otherwise, there was nothing to worry about. Unless Justin and Chloe kept nosing around.

All of this was because of Drew, he thought with a curse as he cleaned his rifle. They should never have let Drew into the deal. But once he'd gotten wind of it, there was no keeping him out. If Drew had come up with the money like he said he would, none of this would be happening. Drew had no one to blame for his death but himself.

He knew they couldn't trust Drew and had argued against bringing him in. But they'd been short a partner, short enough money to make it happen, and Drew had promised he wouldn't let them down.

He thought about the night he went out to the Calhoun ranch to pick up the money. They were so close to making the deal that they could all taste it. He'd been excited maybe for the first time in his life. He would be able to do anything he wanted. He'd been so sure they were going to make it happen and since he had the most invested, he would make the most.

The moment he saw Drew's face that night, he'd known the cocky cowboy hadn't come up with his share. He'd waved off all the man's excuses as he'd tried to still the rage inside him. Drew wanted him to sit down so they could talk about it. Talk about it? Why had they thought they could trust this man?

Here, have a drink, the cowboy had said. *We'll figure something out. You and I can get past all of this.*

He could see his dreams going down the drain and all because of this worthless piece of—

Drew's pistol was within reach. No coincidence there. The cowboy wasn't stupid. He'd known he was in deep trouble. He just hadn't known the extent.

He'd gotten to the gun before Drew. He hadn't even thought about it. He'd just grabbed up the pistol and fired point-blank into the cowboy's chest. He'd been so angry that he'd tossed the gun into the man's lap, never dreaming Drew wasn't going to die within seconds.

Then he'd started toward the door. A bullet whizzed by his head and embedded itself in the wall next to the door.

He hadn't even turned. He'd kept walking, so angry that if he'd gone back he thought he might have emptied the damn gun into Drew's dead body. Nothing like overkill at a time like that. But he'd shown his usual restraint.

He'd parked a good distance away that night and hadn't looked back on the walk to his rig. Unfortunately, he'd been seen, but at the time he hadn't worried about it. He figured no one would believe Nici if she did go to the sheriff. But he knew she wouldn't. She hated the law as much as he did, so he'd kept walking.

When Drew Calhoun's death had been ruled an accident, he'd relaxed. It had felt as if justice had really been served, although he'd had to let go of his dream of being rich and free. He'd thought it was all behind him. The only other person who knew what he'd done besides Nici Kent was his banker—and if anything disturbed his sleep it was knowing that Monte Decker was a man who would crack under even a little pressure.

But after five years, he'd begun to sleep as well as breathe just fine.

Until Chloe Clementine had started looking into Drew's death, dragging Justin into it and making Monte nervous.

He finished cleaning the rifle and placed it back in its spot in the gun safe. Before he closed the door though, he took out a pistol. His work wasn't done, although he hoped he wouldn't have to use the gun. He had another less messy plan.

JUSTIN FELT JUMPY. But who wouldn't be after being shot at earlier? The killer had managed to keep Monte from telling them who he was. Well, it was up to the sheriff now. He was done investigating, he told himself. And Chloe was definitely done although he hadn't told her yet, he thought with a curse.

These past few days he'd come to know her pretty well and yet… They hadn't even kissed. Oh, he'd thought about it on numerous occasions, but none of them had seemed right. He knew he was worried that old magic might not be there. It had been years—and only that one kiss. What if they'd both been mistaken?

The New Year's Eve Masquerade Dance was only forty-eight hours away. He was thinking that might be the perfect time. Maybe by then the sheriff would have Drew and Monte's murderer behind bars. There would be nothing holding Justin back.

Just the thought of kissing Chloe made him

ache with desire. Once he had her in his arms at the dance...

He pushed the thought away as he drove down the street to Nici's house. By now the sheriff would have talked to her. Or maybe not. If McCall was right, Nici might have left town. If she had, it would mean that she was more afraid than she'd told him because she knew who the killer was.

Pulling up to her house she shared with her sisters, he got out and hurried up the unshoveled walk to ring the doorbell. When he heard nothing, he knocked. One of Nici's sisters opened the door, holding a crying toddler in her arms and looking harried.

"Is Nici—"

"She's gone. Cleared out yesterday owing her part of the rent," the sister said bitterly. "If she owes you money, good luck." She closed the door. He could hear her hollering at the toddler to shut up as he walked back to his truck.

Cursing under this breath, he climbed behind the wheel. The sheriff had been right. Nici had run.

BERT WAS TO the point where he was nagging the nurses and doctors about when he could get out of the hospital. So when Justin walked in, he was more than a little glad to see him. But he realized with a surprise that his son wasn't alone.

"Who's this with you?" he asked as a pretty blond, blue-eyed young woman stepped into the room.

"I wanted you to meet Chloe. Chloe Clementine," Justin said.

She stepped to his bed and held out her hand. "It's an honor to meet you."

He shook her hand with a laugh. "An honor, huh? Wait until you get to know me." He glanced at his son and saw the goofy look on Justin's face. The man was in love. He couldn't have been more starry-eyed.

"So how long has this been going on?" Bert asked.

"Chloe and I go way back, but we just recently reconnected," Justin said as he looked over at the blonde. "I've never forgotten her."

Bert nodded. At least his son was serious.

"Chloe is an investigative reporter," his son was saying.

"Or I was until recently. Layoffs. I'm not sure what my plans are right now," she said and looked toward Justin.

Bert knew love when he saw it. He remembered the way he used to look at Mary—and the way she looked back at him. It warmed him inside to think about it. He realized right away that Mary would have liked this young woman. He felt a lump in his throat as he wished she was still around to see this. She would have been thrilled.

"It is nice to meet you," Bert said, proving that he still had manners. "I hope we get to see a lot more of you in the future. Which reminds me, Justin, there's something I need you to do for me."

"I'll let you two talk," Chloe said. "It was nice to meet you, Mr. Calhoun."

"Bert, please." Or maybe one day Dad, he thought as he realized again how much he wanted to live. Was it possible he could live long enough to see grandchildren running around the ranch? It wasn't the dream he'd once had. But he'd had to let go of that dream. Now it seemed there might be a new one. Was he ready for that?

"I'll be out in the waiting room," she said to his son and left.

"Close the door," Bert said and motioned to the chair next to his bed. "I need you to convince the doctor I would be better off at the house. I thought if you told him you were moving back in…" He hesitated. "That isn't why you're here, is it? And it wasn't just to introduce me to your lady friend. What's happened?"

Justin pulled the chair up to the bed. "I'm going to tell you because you're going to hear. But I don't want you getting upset."

He nodded as he lay back against the pillows and told himself his only hope of getting out of this bed was if he learned how to control his damned temper. And yet he wanted to shake the news out of his youngest son. He'd never had patience and it had only gotten worse with the years.

"Monte Decker's been killed."

"What was it—a bank robbery?"

Justin shook his head. "Chloe and I were following a lead in Drew's death. We drove out to his place after finding out that he'd taken what appeared to be an indefinite leave from the bank."

"Monte?" Bert was shaking his head. If Justin was going to tell him that Monte had killed Drew, he was going to have to call bull on it. "If you're going to tell me that he confessed and took his own life—"

"He did confess, but not to Drew's murder. Then he was shot. As far as we can tell, the shooter was in those foothills close to his house."

Bert couldn't believe what he was hearing. "Someone *shot* him?"

His son nodded. "Twice. He was dead before the sheriff arrived."

"And you were afraid this was going to make me have another heart attack?"

"No," Justin said. "It's what Monte confessed to. After what you told me about Drew asking for a large amount of money—"

"Five hundred thousand dollars as if he thought we kept that much out in the barn—"

"I found out that there was a secret group of men trying to buy the mining rights in the Little Rockies before the new EPA regulations went into effect. Had they succeeded they all stood to make a bundle or at least thought they would. Drew was one of the men. Because they had to move quickly, all of them had to come up with their share—"

Bert swore and closed his eyes. He could see Drew almost on his knees begging for the money.

Begging him to come down to the bank and talk to Monte. All Bert had to do was sign a few papers, put the ranch up and let his oldest son walk away with a half million dollars to invest in some fool scheme.

"Are you all right?" Justin said. He'd gotten to his feet and was standing right next to the bed. "Do you want me to call the doctor?"

He could hear the monitor react. His heart was pounding. If he'd given Drew the money... "No, don't call the doctor," he said, opening his eyes. He blinked back the tears, then made a swipe at them. "I'm fine." He wasn't. His heart had broken all over again.

But strange as it was, an already broken heart couldn't seem to break any worse. The monitor sound began to slow again. He'd killed his son.

"You and your lady friend can stop looking for Drew's killer now," he said, surprised how calm he sounded. "We know who killed Drew. I killed him."

"No, Dad, that's not true. You knew him. If you'd given him the money he would have probably tried to double it gambling. He would have screwed up the deal some other way and all that money would be gone."

"And he would have been back for more," Bert said nodding. It was true and he knew it, but right now, none of that helped. Right now he was deep in the if-onlys. "I need to rest for a while." He patted Justin's hand resting on the edge of the bed. "Later, come by and talk to the doctor, will you?" He met his son's gaze. "And I mean it about you moving back to the ranch. Not to take care of your old man. It's where you belong."

Justin's eyes were shiny as he nodded. "Get some rest. I'll be back to spring you."

"I like her," Bert said after him. "Your mother would have too."

JUSTIN TRACKED DOWN his father's doctor at the hospital to see if his father could be released the next morning.

"He is giving the nurses a hard time. I wish I could say we'll be sorry to see him go," the doctor joked.

"That's my father. I'm sorry."

The doctor smiled. "He says you're going to move back into the house. I would suggest having a caregiver on-site as well unless you plan to be there 24/7 at least for a few weeks." He handed Justin a list of names and numbers. "Any of those should be able to handle him."

"So how soon can he leave?"

"Tomorrow morning if he is still doing as well as he is now."

Justin nodded. "I'll start calling the names on the list. I'd like to get that all set up before he comes home."

"Good idea. And best of luck."

"I'll need it until my father can be out on the ranch again doing what he loves," he said.

"I'd tell him not to overdo it but I know I would be wasting my breath. If he makes some changes in his lifestyle, he should be fine. But he has to learn to control his temper."

Justin couldn't see that happening, but he hoped his father surprised him. He walked down the hall to tell his father the good news.

"Not until tomorrow morning?" Bert snapped. "What the hell am I supposed to do in the meantime?"

"Rest. Also I'll be hiring a caregiver to live on-site for a while." He held up his hand to ward off another tirade. "It's the only way the doctor would release you. I'll be there too, but not all the time."

"That woman you brought by…" his father said, frowning.

"Chloe Clementine. Hopefully, you and I will be seeing a lot more of her."

"So it's like that, huh?"

He nodded smiling. "It's like that."

His father finally smiled. "I suppose it wouldn't be so bad having a woman around."

He found Chloe down the hall visiting with an old friend who worked at the hospital. As they left, he felt conflicting emotions. His father wanted him to move back on the ranch. He'd dreamed of the day Bert Calhoun would say that, never believing it would ever happen. He was touched and at the same time…

Mostly he was relieved that his father had taken the news so well.

"I'm glad I got to meet your dad," Chloe said as he drove toward her house.

He smiled over at her. "He liked you. He said my mom would have too."

"That's sweet."

"I like you too," he said, glancing over at her. "We've been so busy..."

She smiled. "The feeling is mutual."

"I can't wait until the dance." He meant that he didn't think he could wait to kiss her until then. That had been his plan. To wait. But being around her like this was killing him.

"Me either," she said of the dance. "I should warn you. My sisters and I were discussing our investigation before you called. We made a list of suspects."

He thought about telling her the two of them were done investigating, but he didn't have the heart. And what would it hurt to see what Chloe and her sisters had come up with? There was a killer out there. If there was any way to find him before he killed again... He just didn't want Chloe risking her life again.

"It comes down to money," Chloe said once she and Justin were inside the warm house. TJ and Annabelle had left a note. They'd both gone to be with their fiancés, leaving Chloe and Justin alone.

She put some music on, poured herself a glass

of wine and opened a beer for him, before they sat down in the living room. She could feel the sexual tension arcing between them and wondered if Justin could too. He seemed nervous as a schoolboy who thought her parents might walk in at any moment.

When their gazes met and held, she felt heat rush to her center. They'd gotten so close. Was he as afraid as she was that if they took it any further, they'd be disappointed?

"So let's see this list you came up with," he said as if needing a diversion.

"Out of the people that Drew knew and hung out with, who had the money to invest?" she asked as Justin took a sip of his beer.

"You're assuming it was his poker-playing buddies, but don't forget about his best friend, CJ Hanson," Justin said as he studied the list they'd made. "His grandfather left him money and CJ, as rough as he is, wasn't dumb enough to blow it. I wouldn't be surprised if he'd invested it."

Chloe added his name to the list. "So the regular poker-playing buddies I know about were Drew Calhoun, Pete Ferris, Al Duncan and Monte Decker. There are others we came up with in town who might have had the money to invest and would have wanted in on the deal, but they didn't travel in the same circles as Drew."

Justin agreed. "You can scratch Al Duncan off the list. He couldn't have come up with the money. But they weren't the only ones who played poker with

Drew. CJ Hanson, his best friend, played occasionally but he probably knew that Drew cheated so was smart enough not to lose his money to him. Blaine Simpson also played with them and our ranch manager, Thane Zimmerman."

"Blaine?" Chloe couldn't help her surprise.

"That was before he found out that Drew had been trying to steal his wife."

He was studying the list. "Wait, there was one more. Your old friend Kelly Locke. He was younger than the rest of them so they probably fleeced him."

Chloe couldn't have been more shocked. "I hope they did." Her heart was pounding. "Well, if you are looking for a killer, I vote for the now-suspended Deputy Kelly Locke."

Justin nodded, his jaw tightening. "He sounds like he's a good candidate but I'd have to put my money on Thane Zimmerman. I didn't tell you, but I found out that he's been stealing from the ranch for years, worse since my father has been distracted. I fired him. He and Drew used to butt heads. There was no love lost between them. I just can't imagine that Thane had that kind of money though."

"Right. I doubt Deputy Locke had the funds either. But it's hard to say since we don't know if he has a rich uncle he could have gotten it from," she said.

Justin put down the list. "What we don't have though is proof. Lots of suspects but no proof. But if all of those on the list had come up with half a million, except Monte who kicked in two hundred thousand, they would have had close to four million dollars. If losing five hundred thousand soured the deal at the last minute, then there must not have been any wiggle room with the finances."

As that conversation waned, Chloe asked, "Did you tell your father what we'd found out?" He nodded. "How'd he take it?"

Justin smiled and shook his head. "Better than I expected. He's anxious to get out of the hospital. He wants me to move back onto the ranch."

She curled her feet under her and sipped her wine. "How do you feel about that?"

"I know it's where I belong, but I'm not sure I'm ready. We'll see." He picked up the list, then put it down again, his gaze going to hers. "I should go. I have a dance coming up and no costume yet. Dawson's mother, though, said not to worry. She's going to help me out."

She grinned as she put down her wineglass and rose with him. "Willie? I can't wait to see what she comes up with for you."

He laughed and shook his head. Moving to the door, he pulled on his coat and boots, then took his Stetson from the hook by the door and settled it on his head. "I would imagine *cowboy*'s been taken." His smile faded. "You sure you'll be all right here by yourself?"

She glanced at the clock on the wall. "My sisters will be back any moment. I'll lock the door behind you. I'll be fine."

He still looked reluctant to leave and she wondered how much of it had to do with a killer on the loose—or this electricity sparking between them. They weren't teenagers. It was only a matter of time before they did a whole lot more than kiss.

And yet he seemed to be holding back.

"I suppose it's too much to hope that the sheriff will have found Drew and Monte's killer before New Year's Eve," he said. "Otherwise, we could be sharing the dance floor with a murderer."

That's if the person who killed both Drew and Monte didn't kill again before then. She knew that was what had him worried. As her sisters drove up, she saw Justin relax. "Talk to you later?"

She nodded and smiled.

Chapter Seventeen

Chloe hoped she could find something to wear to the costume dance. She promised herself she would look at the stores in the morning.

Tired after the day she'd had, she went upstairs, showered and climbed into bed with one of TJ's books. It was just getting to a really scary part when Justin called.

"I hope I didn't wake you," he said.

She put down the book and lay back on her bed. "You didn't. I was reading one of my sister's books and about to scare myself into nightmares, so I'm glad you called."

"You get scared reading a book but not when bullets are flying in your direction?" he asked with a laugh.

She loved the intimate feel of talking late at night on the phone. Their voices were soft and low. She got the feeling that Justin was lying on his bed, as well. "I was scared."

"Are you all right now?"

"Right now, I'm wonderful. All it took was the sound of your voice."

He chuckled at that. "You don't know how hard it was not to touch you at your house earlier."

She felt her heart bump in her chest. This was another thing about these late night phone calls. It was easier to say the things she wanted to. "Why didn't you?"

"You're going to think I'm crazy but I had this idea that we would kiss at the dance. I had this idea that it would be...romantic. Sappy, huh? But I don't think I can wait."

Smiling, she said, "I'm glad to hear that. Are you afraid though that you'll be disappointed?"

"Not a chance. Being around you, I feel as if I've grabbed hold of a live electrical wire. Half the time when I look at you, I'm afraid my heart will beat out of my chest."

She chuckled. "I know the feeling."

He was quiet for a few moments. "I guess I also wanted to take it slow. I've jumped into things before and only managed to mess them up. I don't want to do that with you."

She hugged herself and pressed the phone even tighter to her ear. "I'm glad."

"I should let you get some sleep. I need to pick up my father tomorrow morning at the hospital and take him out to the ranch. I've hired a nurse who will be moving in to one of the guest rooms for the next few weeks. I also need to look around the ranch and see what all needs to be done. At some point, I'll have to hire a new ranch manager."

"You have a lot on your plate right now. If there is anything I can do…"

"Just start the New Year with me on the dance floor."

"Sounds like a plan."

"Are you going to be all right tomorrow?"

"I'll be fine. We told the sheriff everything we know. The killer has no reason to come after us."

"Except for the fact that we're the reason all this has come to light," he pointed out.

"I would think this person is more worried about getting away with the murders he has already committed than getting back at the two of us."

Justin agreed. "He's managed to get away with Drew's murder for five years. So he's not stupid. Stupid would be coming after us."

"Exactly. I have things I need to do too. Like figure out my costume for the dance."

"Something sexy like you."

She smiled. "We'll see." She ached to be in his arms right now under a thick down comforter, cuddled together. And she wanted that kiss badly. She was glad he said he couldn't wait until the dance.

Something told her those original fireworks were still there—actually even more potent because of these days they'd spent together fighting to keep their hands off each other.

"I haven't had time to even think about my costume for the dance and the double wedding is the next day. Would you want to go with me?"

"I'd be honored." They both fell silent until finally he broke the quiet. "Sleep tight. I'll be thinking about you."

"Me too." She listened as he disconnected before she did the same. She smiled at herself in the dark. She was falling in love all over again with Justin T. Calhoun and they hadn't even kissed again yet.

She picked up TJ's book but quickly put it aside again. Instead, she lay on the bed staring at the ceiling and thinking about the good-looking cowboy. Just the thought of him made her heart beat faster: The sound of his voice on the phone tonight had left her tingling inside. She hadn't felt excited like this about anyone in a very long time.

HE OFTEN WONDERED about people. It amazed him that some people thought they were smarter than him. He shook his head as he drove out of town. The moment he realized Nici had left, he'd known he had to go after her. If she'd been smart, she wouldn't have run. Just like Monte. Running had only made him look guilty.

With Nici, running made it clear to him that she'd seen him that night on the Calhoun ranch. And now she'd taken off because he'd killed Monte and she feared she couldn't keep her mouth shut. Or she was worried that he would come looking for her next.

So maybe she wasn't so dumb after all because

he *was* looking for her. And if he was right, he knew where she'd gone. What he didn't understand was why she hadn't sung like a canary the night she'd seen him leaving Drew's cabin. True, she disliked the law—and there was a good chance they wouldn't have believed her. But he thought it was more a case of being guilty herself. He'd witnessed at least part of the fight she'd had with Drew.

If Nici had come forward right away with what she knew, she would have had to admit that she was the one who'd scratched the hell out of Drew before he died. He bet that some of Drew Calhoun's skin was probably still under her nails that night.

So, yes, she had her reasons for keeping her mouth shut. But maybe not so much now. He could guess why she hadn't put the bite on him. Nici wasn't above blackmail. She could have tried to bleed him dry with what she knew. Unless she didn't want to take the chance that he might find out who she was. Was it possible that she didn't realize that he'd seen her the night he killed Drew?

No, he thought as he slowed his pickup for the turnoff ahead, she knew. And now he knew because she'd run. Stupid girl. Now she was going to have to die.

Chapter Eighteen

Nici Kent was holed up in a cabin down in the Snowy Mountains. He'd figured she'd go there since the place belonged to a neighbor. He knew she'd be wary. That's why he'd come at night, parked down the road and walked up the mountain to the cabin. Her small older car was parked partway down the road. Apparently that was as far as she was able to get through the snow.

He was a little winded by the time he reached the dark cabin. It had been a while since he'd done any manual labor. Climbing up a mountain through the deep snow was tougher than he remembered.

No lights shown inside the small structure. He was almost to it when his cell phone rang. Hurriedly taking it from his pocket, he answered, surprised that he'd forgotten to put his phone on vibrate. He'd slipped up and he didn't like that. If he'd been any closer to the cabin, it would have alerted Nici, something he wanted to avoid.

Seeing who was calling, he turned off his phone and repocketed it with a silent curse. He didn't need to deal with the caller right now. What was he saying? He didn't ever want to deal with the caller.

He moved along the side of the cabin. Smoke rose from the chimney into the growing dusk. He wanted this over with quickly so he could get back to Whitehorse.

His hope was that Nici felt safe here. Still, he doubted she would leave the front door open. The back door though was another story since these cabins didn't have running water—especially in the winter. That meant that she would have to use the outhouse up on the hill.

He tried the back door. Locked. Swearing under his breath, he realized that she was more spooked even here in the mountains than he had expected. He thought about waiting her out. Eventually she would have to use the facilities, such as they were.

But he had little patience. He'd already taken the time to drive down here. He couldn't waste any more time with this. He found the power source to the cabin even though it appeared she'd already gone to bed since there were no lights on inside. He cut the power just in case. He'd never minded working in the dark.

He wasn't planning on using the gun. But he pulled it. At the back door, he listened again. No sound from inside. With luck he would finish this and be home before anyone knew he'd been gone.

Gun in hand, he kicked in the back door and burst in.

JUSTIN THOUGHT OF something that had started to worry him and called Chloe right back. "Aren't our costumes supposed to kind of match at the dance?"

She laughed. "I'm sure whatever Willie comes up with for you will be amazing. And mine will just be something sexy."

"I'm sure it will be no matter what you find to wear. By the way, what do I need to wear to your sisters' wedding?"

"It's Montana. Do you own a clean pair of jeans?"

"Got it. No plaid," he joked. "Hell, I might surprise you and show up with a new pair of boots."

"You don't have to get that crazy—"

"Hang on a minute. That's weird, I have another call." He hit the flash button to put Chloe on hold and connect with the other caller.

"Justin!"

He sat straight up in bed. "Nici, what is it?" She was crying so hard, he couldn't understand what she was saying. "Where are you? Nici, tell me where you are. Stay right there. I'm on my way." He cut back to Chloe. "I just got a call from Nici. She's a friend and she's in trouble."

"Pick me up? I'll go with you."

"I'm on my way."

CHLOE WAS DRESSED and waiting at the door when Justin pulled up. She ran out to his pickup and climbed in. "Did she say what had happened?" she asked as he threw the truck into gear and took off down the street.

He drove for a moment without answering. "She was crying so hard I couldn't tell." He glanced at her. "There's something I should have told you before this. Nici and I have been friends for a long time. At one time, well, we were more than that."

"I know."

"I can't help being protective of her. Nici, well, she's been her own worst enemy. I've been worried about her for the past five years. When Monte was killer earlier…"

Chloe heard five years. Then Monte. "Was Nici…" She wasn't sure what to ask, just that it was clear it had something to do with Drew and his death. She held her breath.

Justin was busy driving as snowflakes fell in a dizzying rush that the wipers were fighting to keep up with. "Nici was there the night Drew was killed."

"She didn't—"

"No, but I've long suspected that she didn't just see who killed Drew—but the killer saw her."

"She didn't tell you who she saw?"

He shook his head. "Believe me I've tried to talk to her about this."

"Why wouldn't she have told the sheriff?"

"This happened before you came to live in Whitehorse. Nici's father was killed by the local sheriff. Her father was drunk and, threatening to kill the sheriff at that time, rushed the man… Nici has had a problem with the law ever since."

Chloe stared at the snow-covered road ahead. "You think the killer found her." She glanced over at Justin and could see how worried he was. "Did she say if she was injured?"

He shook his head. "All I got out of her was that she'd be waiting for us at the Hayes turnoff."

JUSTIN PULLED OFF at what was once a trailer park. Now there was a small store there along with some abandoned cars and other discarded equipment. The store was closed and from what he could tell, there was no one around.

Nor did he see Nici's old car. He pulled in, cut his lights and pulled out his phone. It wasn't snowing quite as hard as earlier, but it was still hard to see if anyone was coming up the highway. He started to call Nici when his phone buzzed with a text.

I'm here. Pull up to the store and cut your engine.

He started to do as she said, when Chloe laid a hand on his arm.

"What if that isn't her texting? What if someone has her phone?"

Justin looked at her for a moment, before he texted back.

What's your favorite beer?

Nothing happened for a long minute before an emoji appeared along with the words Anything you're buying.

He smiled over at Chloe, then pulled closer to the store and cut his engine. Snowy darkness closed in around them. They waited. He stared out at the darkness through the falling snow, all his senses on alert. Something bad had happened. Maybe Nici had gotten away. Or maybe she wasn't alone out there as she thought she was.

When she came running up to the pickup, he jumped and Chloe let out a startled cry. She quickly opened her door and slid over in the bench seat to let Nici in.

The moment the door slammed, she said, "Go! Get me out of here!"

He hurriedly started the motor and pulled out onto the highway again.

Chloe had pulled off her coat and wrapped it around Nici even against her protests.

"Are you hurt?" Justin asked glancing over at her. There was blood on her cheek and her left eye was swollen. She looked more frightened than hurt.

They drove in silence for ten miles. Finally, Justin said, "Tell me what happened." He wasn't sure Nici would, but he had to know what they were up against.

"What do you think happened?" she demanded.

"He came after me. And don't even bother to say I told you so."

"Where is he now?" Chloe asked.

Nici shrugged. "I stabbed him. For all I know he's back there bleeding to death."

Justin swore. "You could have been killed."

"Really?" Nici laughed but sounded closer to tears. "I never thought of that."

"We're going to the sheriff."

"No!" Nici cried. "You do that and I'm dead."

"I don't do that and you're dead," Justin snapped. "Nici, you can't keep running from this. You have to tell the sheriff who the killer is."

Nici laughed—this time it ended in sobs. "That's the problem, Justin. I didn't get a good look at the man that night. I couldn't see his face, but he *saw* me. I'd hoped maybe he hadn't recognized me."

He stared over at her for a moment before turning back to his driving. "But you saw him tonight."

Nici shook her head. "It was dark. He must have cut the power. All I know is that he is big and strong. If I hadn't stabbed him…"

Chloe put her arm around the young woman. "Take her to my house," she said. Nici started to protest again. "You'll be safe there until we decide what to do."

Chapter Nineteen

The next morning, Chloe woke to the sounds of her sisters talking in the kitchen. She quickly showered and dressed and went downstairs. When she walked into the kitchen to the smell of coffee and cinnamon rolls, she said, "Where's Nici?"

"Nici?" TJ said and looked at Annabelle. "Why would Nici—"

But Chloe didn't stick around to let her finish. She rushed back through the living room to the second downstairs bedroom where she and Justin had put the young woman last night. The bed was unmade, the room empty.

She swore, turning to find both of her sisters looking at her questioningly. As she called Justin, she started to fill them in.

"Hello?"

"Nici's gone."

Justin swore. "I was afraid of that."

"She must have left in the middle of the night. What are we going to do?"

"I'm going to the sheriff."

"Do you want me to come?" she asked.

"No, I'll handle it. But if you hear from her…"

"I'll call." She disconnected and saw that her sisters were impatiently waiting to know what was going on. She told them an abbreviated version.

"She stabbed the man?" TJ cried. "And you didn't call the sheriff?"

"She was too scared. We were afraid she would run again."

Annabelle raised an eyebrow. "Well, it appears she ran anyway."

Chloe felt sick. Nici was out there somewhere and unless she'd killed the man who'd attacked her…

"We have dress fittings," Annabelle said. "Are you going to be all right here by yourself?"

She nodded. "I'll be fine." But as she watched her sisters drive off, Chloe realized this was her last day to get a costume since the dance was tonight. She'd been so busy, she'd lost track of time.

Once the stores opened, she headed uptown to find herself a costume for the dance. It was another snowy day but she didn't mind. She was worried about Nici, but the young woman had survived this long on her wits. She could only hope that sometime during the night Nici had realized going to the sheriff was the smart thing to do.

Justin would be down there now, telling the sheriff what he knew. If the man Nici had stabbed was dead… Then it was all over. Nici would be safe. They all would be safe.

Her cell phone rang. Justin. "Hello, did you tell the sheriff?"

"Nici was picked up last night. She's in a cell at the jail. Apparently she left your house and closed one of the bars. She was so drunk, the bartender called the sheriff's office. They put her in the drunk tank."

She breathed a sigh of relief. Nici was safe. She had to shake her head though. Nici's idea of handling what had happened was to get drunk at the local bar? "Did you tell the sheriff everything?"

"I did. Nici will hate me, but I had to."

"I know. You're a good friend."

He said nothing. "The sheriff is headed down to the mountains to check out the cabin where Nici had been staying. This could be over before the dance tonight."

"I hope so."

"I'm on my way to get a costume," she said.

"Remember, sexy like you."

"How can I forget?"

"Chloe, be careful. It won't be over until whoever tried to kill Nici is caught or found dead."

"Hopefully, we'll hear soon." She disconnected, her spirits buoyed by just the sound of Justin's voice. Nici was safe. Now if the sheriff found the killer dead in the cabin where Nici had been staying…

She couldn't help but think about Justin. The

memory of her conversation with him on the phone last night warmed her. She'd wondered why he hadn't tried to kiss her. Now she knew. He wanted to as badly as she wanted him to.

The dance was tonight and yet he'd said he couldn't wait any longer. She couldn't wait to see him either. Smiling to herself, she walked the few blocks to the center of town. Holiday music played in the stores as she passed. She found herself smiling and singing along. Had she ever felt like this?

In the clothing store, she found some things that she thought might work and tried them on. She smiled to herself in the mirror. Justin had said she should get a sexy costume for the dance. She wondered if this would be sexy enough for him as she checked out her reflection.

She was glad that she'd worked out before coming to Whitehorse. The black leggings fit like a glove, accenting her long legs and tight round derriere. The silky, formfitting black top zipped just high enough that she wouldn't be picked up for indecency.

"Who am I?" she asked the clerk as she came out of the dressing room to stand before the store mirror.

"Anyone you want to be. Catwoman? Or some unknown crime fighter? Your choice." Because of this yearly event, stores often carried costume items.

Chloe laughed when the woman suggested a cape and a whip. "Why not?" She chose a silver mask with rhinestones that hid most of her face. "This is going to be so much fun." She'd been thinking that maybe she would tell Justin she'd meet him at the dance and he would have to find her.

Excited and happy with her costume, she'd come out of the store and started walking back to the house when she passed an older, unoccupied brick building. She was almost past it and the next also-empty building when Kelly Locke stepped out.

She let out a startled cry as she realized he must have been waiting for her. He grabbed her before she could react and pulled her down the narrow opening between the two buildings.

"You and I have some unfinished business," Kelly said as he caged her against the wall. She tried to get past his arms on each side of her, but he blocked her with his body. "That phone trick the other day on the highway. You got me suspended from my job."

"What did you think was going to happen?" she demanded. "You broke the taillight on my sister's car."

"You didn't have that on your phone."

She said nothing. The sheriff had believed her, that's all that mattered.

"You have no idea who you're messing with," he ground out between gritted teeth.

"That's just it," she said. "I'm not messing with you. I want nothing to do with you. You need to leave me alone and get over whatever your problem is."

He shook his head. "Whatever my problem is? *You're* my problem. You butt into other people's business. I tried to warn you that it could get you hurt. You have no idea who you're messing with."

She shook her head, her anger rising. She hated feeling this vulnerable. He was a big man and had always used his strength and size to get what he wanted. He was a classic bully.

But back in high school all she'd seen was his good looks and the fact that he was a hotshot athlete. That was one of the problems with small towns. Kelly had been a big fish in a small pond. It had fed his already overblown ego. The first time he'd noticed little Chloe Clementine she'd been so honored...

"You think you're too good for this town and for me, but I remember when you would have done anything just to be seen with me." He smirked at her.

It was true. She'd never had a boyfriend. Not a real, honest to goodness boyfriend who gave her his class ring to wear. She'd wanted that desperately before her high school years were over. And to be Kelly Locke's girlfriend...

Her heart had pounded when he put his arm around her at school. He would walk past in the lunchroom and steal a cookie from her plate, and wink and grin at her. He would point at her from the football field and her face would heat, knowing everyone was looking at her. Everyone knew she was his girl.

Until she kissed Justin Calhoun.

That bubble she'd been floating around in being

Kelly's girl popped that day. She couldn't explain it, but she suddenly saw Kelly in a different light. And not a positive one. All his male cockiness seemed silly next to a big strong cowboy like Justin, who had been a few years older and already out of school. He'd been already a man.

Kelly on the other hand, she'd realized, no longer enchanted her. He was immature. He was also a lousy boyfriend. She'd felt as if with one kiss, she'd grown up. She'd wanted more. She and Kelly were history.

To say he hadn't taken it well was an understatement.

"You can't be serious," he'd said and laughed, thinking it was a joke. "You breaking up with me." He'd laughed again before realizing he was the only one laughing. "You think you can do better?" He'd snorted. "Seriously?"

She'd tried to explain that she just wanted to move on, but he'd gotten nastier until she'd finally said, "Yes, I know I can do better."

"I'll ruin you. One word from me and no one will ever take you out again. I can destroy you."

She'd walked away with him yelling obscenities at her. Then he'd done exactly what he'd said he would do. He'd told his friends lies. He'd ruined her reputation. He'd made her a pariah. She'd hidden her pain from everyone—even her sisters.

Just being this close to Kelly made her skin crawl. He'd been so cruel to her because she'd rejected him.

And now she'd rejected him again. Only she was no longer a naïve high school girl who'd kissed a boy and believed in happy endings.

She knew how dangerous it was to cross Kelly Locke.

He still had his arms on each side of her, his body so close she felt she couldn't breathe. She kept hoping someone would walk by and see them so she could scream and get away. But this part of town was off the beaten path.

"Actually, I'm glad I ran into you," she said, realizing what she had to do.

That took him by surprise. He leaned back a little and she felt her first ray of hope. He gave her a cheesy grin. "You are?"

"I wanted to ask you about the secret group of investors who were going to buy the mining rights up at Zortman before the new EPA regulations went through."

He drew back even farther. "What?" He seemed to have thought that she was glad to see him for another reason. Certainly not this one. "Who? What are you talking about?"

Kelly Locke was a terrible liar. She'd just bet Drew and the rest of his poker buddies had taken the fool to the cleaners.

"Exactly. I didn't think you knew anything about it. I told my sisters, 'Kelly doesn't have that kind of money. He couldn't come up with even two hundred thousand to be a minor investor—let alone more than that."'

"The hell you say!" he snapped. "Just shows that you don't know what you're talking about. I have money. A whole lot of money. I wasn't one of the minor investors. I was one of the big ones, seven hundred and fifty thousand."

She gave him a disbelieving look. "Where would you get that kind of money?"

He huffed. "My mother's family had money and I was my aunt's favorite. She put it in a trust but Monte said he'd give me a loan for seven hundred and fifty big ones against it. So there, smart girl."

"Still you couldn't have been the biggest investor," she said.

His smugness dropped a notch or two. "Maybe not the biggest but the second!" He'd puffed out his chest, straightening. "So what do you think about me now?" He'd moved back just enough.

Chloe brought her knee up with all the force she could muster. It caught him between his legs. She gave him a shove that sent him sprawling on the ground. He doubled up, rolling to his side as he gasped and groaned in agony.

She hurriedly stepped away knowing that she'd probably made things worse. But look what she'd learned. She would just have to watch her back even closer now.

Chapter Twenty

After picking up his costume, Justin stopped by the sheriff's office. He'd planned to change at Chloe's. He couldn't wait to see her. He couldn't wait to hold her in his arms, let alone kiss her. They'd both been waiting. Tonight would tell the tale. It surprised him that he was only a little nervous and that was more about his dancing skills than anything else.

But first he had to be sure that Nici was okay. Sheriff Crawford motioned him into her office and offered him a chair.

"How is Nici?"

"She's under protective custody."

Justin knew at once what that meant. "You didn't find the man she said she stabbed."

"No, but we found blood and there was evidence of a struggle that matches what Nici told us," McCall said. "We're running the DNA on the blood hoping for a match. Meanwhile, we're also checking any medical facilities in the area if he tried to get help."

"I'd hoped you had him," Justin said. "She told

you she believes he's the man she saw leaving Drew's cabin that night?"

"She did, but she didn't get a good look at him that night or last night," the sheriff said. "She swears she can't ID him. All she said was that he was big and strong."

He nodded. "I'm glad you're keeping her safe."

"We'll find him. If he's injured badly…"

"And if he's not?"

"We have the list you gave us. We're going down it to see if any of the men who might have been involved in the mining deal with Drew have been injured. It just takes time."

"I know. I'm sorry I couldn't get Nici to come to you sooner."

"She's lucky to be alive. She's also lucky to have you for a friend," McCall said.

Justin rose from his chair saying, "I have a dance to get to. I can't keep my date waiting." As he left the sheriff's department, he called Chloe.

"I'm on my way. I was hoping I could change at your place?"

"Sure. I had thought we might want to meet at the dance but I can't wait that long. Any word from the sheriff on the man Nici said she stabbed?"

"I'm just leaving the sheriff's department now. Nici is in protective custody. They didn't find the man." Chloe fell silent. "The sheriff said there was blood. He probably didn't get far. They'll find him. See you soon."

As CHLOE CAME down the steps, her sisters hooted and hollered. "Is this outfit too much?"

"For you? No way," Annabelle said. "You look hot."

She looked to TJ who smiled and gave her a thumbs-up. Her sisters were in their costumes, as well. Annabelle was a swashbuckler. TJ a bookworm, a costume she'd had to explain to Chloe.

"Dawson and Silas are meeting us at the dance," TJ said.

"Justin should be here any moment, so don't wait on us. Go! We'll be right behind you," she told them.

They hesitated. "After what you told us happened earlier..." TJ looked to Annabelle. "Maybe we should wait."

"If Kelly is even walking right, he isn't going to come over here. Right now he is only suspended from work. I don't think he's stupid enough to try anything else. Actually, I suspect he might be running scared. He didn't mean to tell me what he did in that alleyway."

"But you still don't know who killed Drew and Monte," TJ pointed out unnecessarily. "That person is still out there."

"Bleeding," Chloe said.

"Angry and possibly feeling as if he has nothing to lose," her sister argued. "You and Justin stirred all this up after five years. Drew's killer thought he'd gotten away with it and now he's injured, maybe dying."

She knew TJ had a good point, but she didn't want to think about it tonight. She wanted to think only about Justin and being in his arms on the dance floor. And finally getting that kiss. She said as much to her sisters.

"You haven't even kissed yet?" Annabelle cried.

"We're waiting. It's sweet."

Her sister raised a brow. "It's putting a lot of pressure on The Kiss when you finally do lock lips," Annabelle pointed out.

"Thank you for that."

"Just sayin'."

"Just say goodbye," Chloe said, going to the door and opening it. "I'll see you at the dance." She turned off her phone and tossed it on the table. This costume didn't allow her to take her cell phone—not that she would need it. Everyone would be at the dance.

After they finally left, she looked at the time. Justin was late. She tried not to worry about that. But she also couldn't ignore what TJ had said.

A few minutes after her sisters had driven away, she heard the sound of footfalls on the porch and smiled in anticipation and relief.

She hurried to the door, her smile widening as she threw it open—and then fading as she saw that it wasn't Justin at all.

JUSTIN STEPPED OUT of the sheriff's office and walked back to where he'd left his pickup parked earlier. He'd had to pick up his costume and was running late, so he'd left the costume in his pickup and walked the two blocks to the sheriff's office rather than drive through the deep snow. It was hard enough to find a place to park with the New Year's crowds still out and about.

Snow still fell in a silent white shroud. He stopped to breathe the icy air with expectation. He couldn't wait to see Chloe and for this night to begin. It already felt magical.

He'd hoped Drew and Monte's killer would have been found and that all this was finally over. But he wasn't going to let that spoil his evening, he told himself.

As he neared his pickup, he saw at once that one of his tires was flat. He started to get out what he needed to change the tire, thinking it was only going to make him more late. He tried Chloe's number. It went straight to voice mail.

That seemed strange since he'd just talked to her. He noticed something he hadn't seen earlier. Tracks in the snow where someone had knelt down next to the flat tire. Not just flat, he realized as he bent down to inspect it. The tire had been slashed. Heart in his throat, he turned and ran toward her house, praying he reached her in time.

Chapter Twenty-One

"Blaine?" Chloe said in surprise. He was dressed in a US Marine uniform. "I thought you were Justin." She looked past him to the street, but didn't see his vehicle. There was snow on his hat and the shoulders of his uniform. Had he walked from the dance?

"Actually, Justin's who I'm looking for. I thought he might be here. Looks like you're headed for the dance. I'm meeting Patsy there. But I ran into some trouble."

"I expect him any moment. Is there something I can do?"

"Would you mind if I waited for him?" Blaine said taking off his hat and shaking off the snow.

"Oh, I'm sorry, come in out of the cold." She stepped back to let him in.

Blaine looked at his watch. "Your date is running late."

"He called just a few minutes ago and said he was on his way. Maybe he ran into trouble." That thought did nothing to relieve her growing anxiety. She'd offered Blaine a seat, but he'd said he'd rather stand. He seemed nervous, making her even more so.

She told herself he might be here to tell Justin something about Drew and the mining deal. If Blaine had been one of them, after Monte being killed, he would probably be rattled like the others. He might be running scared that the killer among them would be coming after him.

"Can I get you something to drink?" she asked, needing to do something.

"That would be great. I'm just anxious to get to the dance. I don't like to keep my wife waiting."

She could understand that. "Isn't this something that can wait until after the dance?"

"No," he said, his gaze meeting hers for a moment. "I'm afraid it can't."

When he said no more, Chloe went into the kitchen to grab a bottle of beer out of the refrigerator. She was thinking she could really use one too when she was relieved to hear footfalls on the porch. "Do you mind getting that?" she called to Blaine as she grabbed a second bottle. She figured Justin might want one.

But as she turned to look back into the living room, she was shocked to see Kelly Locke standing there. She was even more shocked when she heard Blaine say, "You're late. You take care of her. I'll wait for Justin. Hurry. I want this fast and clean."

Chloe dropped the beer bottles as Kelly charged into the kitchen. The bottles hit the floor, beer going everywhere. She stumbled back, but Kelly was on her before she could even think about reaching for a weapon to hold him off.

"Going to get what you deserve," he whispered as he covered her mouth with a horrible-smelling rag. She didn't even get a chance to scream let alone fight as the room began to blur. As she was drifting off, she heard Blaine say, "Your pickup out back? Take her that way. I'll meet you as soon as I'm through here."

JUSTIN RACED UP the porch steps. He didn't bother to knock. All his instincts told him that Chloe was in trouble. Rationally, he'd told himself on the race to her house that it could have been kids acting up before the end of the year who'd slashed the tire. But in his gut, he knew better. A tire slashed tonight of all nights after what had been going on with them? No way.

He burst in and came to a skidding stop. Blaine, dressed in his Marine's uniform, was standing in the living room, clearly waiting for him, a gun in his hand. Chloe was nowhere to be seen. "Where's—"

"She's safe. For the moment." Blaine shook his head. "You should have stayed away." He sounded sad.

Justin felt his stomach drop. "I didn't want it to be you."

Blaine shrugged. "If there is one thing I learned in the military it was that it has to be someone. I've been butchering cattle since I was a boy. After a while, death is no big deal."

He noticed that Blaine seemed to be favoring his left side. "But killing people—"

"It isn't all that different."

"You must have been the large investor," Justin said. "Why? You've got your family's big ranch."

Blaine chuckled. "You think I want to spend the rest of my life working that ranch? I'm sick of cows and driving miles to pick up tractor parts and feeding all winter not to mention calving in freezing weather."

"You could have sold and left."

"My father would never allow that. He's down in Arizona with his new wife living off half what I make at the ranch. I had a chance to get out and your brother…" He shook his head. "Ancient history. Where's Nici?"

"In jail. Safe from you."

Blaine nodded. "So she's already told the sheriff everything."

He nodded, letting the big cowboy think that the sheriff was now looking for him. Maybe he would run instead of finishing what he'd started. "Blaine, it's over."

"Not quite. I just saw the sheriff. Nici didn't talk. I can handle her. But the two of you…" Blaine shook his head again. "Let's go." The man motioned toward the front door with his gun.

"I'm not going anywhere until you tell me where Chloe is."

"Deputy Locke has her so I suggest we get moving. You don't want him alone with her very long, do you?"

Justin had no choice. "If he touches a hair on her head—"

"Right. Maybe I'll let you kick his ass before I kill you."

"COME ON, BABY," Kelly cooed next to her ear. "Wake up. We can have some fun before your boyfriend gets here."

Chloe kept her eyes closed. She'd already felt his hand on her breast over the top of her sweater. Fortunately, he apparently drew the line at raping her while she was knocked out. A scumbag with morals, she thought and tried not to shudder. She couldn't keep pretending to be out. He wasn't stupid.

He lifted her sweater.

"Ouch!" She let out a cry as he pinched her bare side hard and she tried to smack him.

Kelly let out a satisfied laugh. "That's what I thought. Blaine said the drug on the cloth only lasted for a little while. You've probably been awake this whole time."

She pretended to be groggier than she was as she sat up. "Where am I?" They appeared to be in some sort of makeshift building. There were cracks be-

tween the boards where she could see outside. It was
still snowing. Some of the snow had drifted in to
form shapes on the dirt floor.

"Just a little lean-to Blaine keeps for this sort of
thing, apparently." Kelly glanced around. "I hope
he hurries. I'm getting cold. What about you, sweetheart? Why don't I warm you up?"

Chloe found herself on a bench. She swung her
legs over the side to lean back against the wood wall.
She could feel the wind blowing in through a crack
behind her. It was cold in here. She could see her
breath and Kelly's.

As she sat all the way, she noticed that he kept his
distance. Smart man. She would bet he was still sore
from the last time. But not sore enough. "What have
you gotten yourself involved in, Kelly?"

"What's it to you? You don't give a damn about
me."

She sat up a little. He took a wary step back. As
she talked she assessed the inside of the shack looking for something she could use as a weapon. The
only thing within reach was an old singletree horse
collar. It was about two feet long, with a couple
inches thick of hardwood with metal at the edges.
This one, which looked like an antique, had a metal
ball on the end of it.

"You do realize that Blaine is going to kill me,
don't you?"

"You only have yourself and Justin to blame for
it," he snapped. "You think any of us wanted this?"

"You can stop this. You're a sheriff's deputy."

He scoffed at that. "It wasn't that long ago you were making fun of me. Now you want me to save you?"

"Save yourself. Do you really think he's going to let you live with what you know?" she demanded.

Kelly looked a little worried for a moment, but covered it with bravado. "Blaine and I are in this together. I was there for him when he called and said that bimbo Nici Kent had stabbed him. I was the one who got him the supplies he needed and helped stitch him up. We're friends."

She shook her head. "You're kidding yourself. A man like Blaine doesn't have friends. This is all going to come out and when it does, you will go down for your part in it. Right now, you aren't in that deep, but if you wait…" She thought she was making some headway with him. He looked nervous as if realizing she might be right.

But then they both heard the sound of an approaching vehicle.

Chloe cursed under her breath. At least she'd kept Kelly at bay. But that didn't mean she was out of the woods. Now that she and Justin knew that he was behind Drew's murder and Monte's, as well…

The door to the lean-to groaned open. Justin stumbled in, followed directly behind by Blaine and the gun in his hand.

"Are you all right?" Justin asked, quickly moving to her.

She nodded. "I'm okay." But they both knew it was temporary.

"I did as you said," Kelly quickly told Blaine. Chloe could see that he was scared of Blaine and probably had been even without her warning him about the man.

"Did Locke lay a hand on you?" Blaine asked her.

She glanced at Kelly. He looked like he might pee his pants. The hand on the breast aside, she said, "No."

"Good. Then you don't get to beat him up," Blaine said to Justin.

Kelly grinned as if he thought Blaine was joking. He looked almost giddy with relief, but also anxious to get out of this situation. He wasn't that much shorter or stockier than Blaine and yet he seemed small next to him. In a fair fight, Kelly would lose. Just as Drew had.

"I guess you're done, then, Deputy Locke," Blaine said.

Kelly started for the door. Chloe saw the moment he realized Blaine wasn't just blocking the door. The big cowboy wasn't going to let him live. The look on his face was one of shock and disappointment.

The report of the gun sounded like a canon going off in the small space. The second shot was on the heels of the first. Kelly let out a cry and grabbed his chest. He looked down at the blood rushing from between his fingers with both shock and alarm. Taking a step toward Blaine, he stumbled and fell face first to the cold dirt.

JUSTIN HELD CHLOE, his mind whirling as he franti-
cally searched for a way out of this for the two of
them. At the sound of the gunshots he'd taken a step
away from her as if to rush Blaine. But she'd held
him back.

"Not now," she'd whispered. He realized that she
had pulled a singletree over to her side, the move-
ment and sound covered by the gunfire. She kept the
two feet of hardwood and metal hidden next to her.

It had been impulsive even thinking of rushing
the man, Justin realized belatedly. He had no doubt
that he would have been shot. What was so terrify-
ing was how cool and calm Blaine had been since
the beginning. No wonder he hadn't suspected him.
He'd expected the killer to be more nervous in fear
of being caught.

Now he tried to find that same kind of calm. He
would need it if he hoped to get Chloe out of this
mess. When he'd come in, he'd taken in what there
might be to fight their way out of this shack. He
didn't particularly want to die here and he really
didn't want to die until he'd kissed this woman.

"I should have kissed you," he said to Chloe. She
sat on a bench. Under it, he'd spotted an old hay
hook. Now as he moved closer to her, he moved the
hay hook out some from under the bench with the
toe of his boot.

She smiled at him and reached up with her left
hand to touch his face.

"This is sweet, but I have a dance to get to,"

Blaine said as he took a step toward them. "This is nothing personal."

"Then you don't mind giving us just a minute to have a New Year's Eve kiss," Chloe said, sounding near tears. She stood up and started to throw her arms around Justin.

He saw what she was planning to do and knew there was no stopping her. All he could do was hope that it bought them the time he needed.

She came up with the heavy wood and metal of the antique singletree. He could tell that it was heavier than she'd thought. As she started to throw her arms around him, he ducked, bending down to pick up the hay hook as she swung the length of wood and metal with the large metal ball on the end.

Justin heard it make contact at the same time he heard the sound of a gunshot boom. He grabbed the hay hook, shoved Chloe aside and swung around, leading with the deadly sharp hook at the end.

The hook caught Blaine in the side and tore across into his stomach as Justin lunged for the gun. The cowboy let out of howl of pain and was distracted just long enough that Justin was able to get his hand on the weapon and wrench it free. He stepped back and raised the gun, fearing Blaine wasn't finished.

Blaine pulled the hay hook from where it had stopped at the middle of his stomach. He wavered for a moment before throwing the hook aside. Holding his already wounded side, he charged him like the crazed man he was.

Justin fired three shots before Blaine dropped at his feet. It had all happened within seconds.

A cold silence, like the snow that blanketed the world outside the shack, followed. He rushed to Chloe. She lay on the ground next to the bench. For a heart-stopping moment, he feared she'd been shot.

He pulled her to him, thankful his prayers had been answered. As he wiped the tears running down her face, he held her tight as he called the sheriff.

Chapter Twenty-Two

The sun was coming up by the time the sheriff dropped Chloe off at her house. As she walked in, her sisters came careening down the stairs to wrap her in their arms. Until that moment, she'd held it together fairly well. But now, she let the tears come. They were tears of relief and sadness and exhaustion.

"You never made it to the dance," Annabelle said. "When we got the call—we were so scared."

She nodded as they led her over to the couch. Both of them were in their Christmas flannel pj's—a present to the three of them from Willie, Dawson's mom. Annabelle's had reindeer on them. TJ's had Santa and Chloe's had adorable elves. She wished she had hers on right now, she thought as she wiped her eyes.

"Tell us everything," Annabelle said.

"Can't you see that she isn't in any shape to talk right now?" TJ said. "She needs to get some sleep."

Chloe smiled at her sisters. "I am exhausted but I know the two of you. If I don't tell you I'll sense both of you waiting impatiently and I won't be able to get any sleep."

She told them everything. They listened horrified and relieved. They hugged her again and insisted she go to bed. It didn't take much encouragement. Upstairs she pulled on her flannel pj's covered in elves and curled up under the down comforter. She had barely closed her eyes and she was out.

Chloe woke to the smell of bacon and pancakes. She showered, dressed and went downstairs, her stomach growling. She couldn't remember the last time she ate. Her sisters were at the table. They dished her up a plate and she ate as if she hadn't eaten in a month.

"It didn't hurt her appetite at least," TJ quipped.

Annabelle poured her some orange juice, which she quickly downed after a murmured thank-you.

It wasn't until she finished, that she realized what day it was. "Oh no, it's your wedding day!" She looked from one sister to the other and back. "I've ruined your weddings."

"Seriously?" TJ said. "You're blaming yourself for almost dying at the hands of a madman?"

"But your weddings!" she cried.

"We put them off," Annabelle said. "It's just fine."

"It's not." Chloe looked at the clock on the wall. "There's time. I can change. You can get into your dresses—"

"We aren't getting married today," TJ said. "So stop."

"No, we can't let this—"

"We have another reason we want to wait," Annabelle said trying to suppress a grin. TJ shot her a warning look and her youngest sister quickly sobered.

"What's going on?" Chloe asked searching their faces for answers and getting none.

The doorbell rang.

"I wonder who that could be?" Annabelle said and giggled.

"What are you two up to?" she demanded.

"You should get that," TJ said.

Getting up she went to the door and blinked in surprise. Justin stood on the porch dressed in a tux complete with top hat and cane.

"I went for vintage Hollywood for the dance," he said. "What do you think?"

She thought he couldn't look more handsome and said as much. He smiled and reached for her hand. "Where are we going?" she asked as he pulled her outside. The day was bright and clear and cold. Snow crystals hung in the air.

"Remember our first kiss?" he asked.

Chloe laughed. "You mean our only kiss?"

"It was on a day like this."

"It was."

He drew her close. "I'm not letting another day go by."

She looked up into his handsome face as he leaned toward her. She held her breath suddenly afraid. She'd been dreaming about this moment for years.

His lips brushed over hers. She breathed in the frosty air as he pulled her against him, wrapping her in his arms and kissed her.

She'd thought she'd had the perfect winter kiss, but this one proved her wrong. This kiss surpassed even the first one. The icy cold air around them. Puffs of frosty white breaths intermingling. Warm lips touching, tingling as they met.

Justin lifted her up off her feet as the kiss deepened. She lost herself in him and the snowy morning. He set her down slowly, but she swore her feet were still not touching the ground. She felt as if she was floating.

"It seems the magic is still there," he said with a chuckle.

She laughed, ice crystals sparkling all around her. The sky overhead was a deep dark blue that seemed filled with endless possibilities.

He looked so serious. "I love you, Chloe. I know this seems sudden but at the same time, it seems as if I've been waiting to say that for years." His blue gaze locked with hers. "Chloe, I came back to Whitehorse because of you."

THE DAYS THAT followed were a blur. It all came out about the mining deal and who was involved and why Drew Calhoun was killed. Monte Decker's body was cremated and a distant aunt came to collect his ashes. Kelly Locke was buried at the cemetery. The turnout was sparse.

But it was Blaine Simpson who had everyone shaking their heads. "He was such a likeable cowboy," they said. "And his poor wife." Everyone felt bad for Patsy. They would have taken her casseroles and flowers and held her hand, but she left the day after she was given the news about her husband.

"What happens to the ranch?" Chloe asked.

"Blaine's father is putting it on the market," Justin said. "Ironic, huh? He was so determined to keep it in the family when all the time Blaine just wanted out from under it."

"Is that how you feel about your family ranch?" she asked.

He laughed. "Not at all. I always wanted to ranch it. Drew was the one who felt tied down." Justin had sobered. "How do you feel about living on a ranch in Montana?"

"I would love it."

"You wouldn't miss the newspaper business?"

"That business is dying. But thanks to computers and the internet I can work anywhere. I would imagine I'll always find stories I want to do…"

Justin had smiled. "I could live with that."

They'd spent every moment together since that kiss. It had been incredible. She would lie in his arms at night and wonder how she'd gotten so lucky.

Justin was easygoing. He laughed a lot and got her sense of humor. He'd often break into song and she would join him. They found out that they liked the same food, the same kind of houses, the same kind of furniture. Neither of them was a morning person. It was almost as if they were made for each other.

Epilogue

"A triple wedding? Whose insane idea was this?" Chloe demanded and then laughed as she looked at her sisters. Their wedding gowns were so beautiful. Each of them had chosen their dream dress. The dresses couldn't have been more different.

"You two look amazing," she said as tears blurred her eyes.

"Do not cry. You'll ruin your makeup," TJ ordered, looking a little misty-eyed herself.

"Are we really doing this?" Annabelle asked looking so excited she seemed to vibrate.

"We're doing this," Chloe said. "Three sisters."

"Three sisters in love," Annabelle said grinning.

Even TJ smiled at that. Chloe had never seen her looking happier. It was true what they said about pregnant women, she practically glowed. It had been TJ's and Annabelle's idea to move the wedding to February fourteenth.

"Valentine's Day?" Chloe had cried. "Why would you want to do that?"

"It's a day of love," Annabelle had said.

"You will be celebrating your anniversary with the world," she'd pointed out.

"Nothing wrong with that," TJ had said with a laugh. "It will give Silas time to finish our cabin so when we come back from our honeymoon, we can move in." She'd patted her stomach even though she was far from showing. "We have a nursery to get ready. Silas is beside himself with excitement."

"Unlike you," Chloe had laughed. TJ was going to make such a good mother.

"It will give Dawson time to finish the addition out on the ranch," Annabelle had said, then looked sad for a moment. "Originally it was going to be for the two of you to have a nice place to stay when you visited. But now..." Suddenly her face had lit up. "But now at least one of the rooms is going to be a nursery."

"Are you—"

"Not yet," she'd said. "But we're not planning to wait. Fingers crossed. I can't wait to be pregnant."

Now Annabelle turned to look in the mirror. "I'm not showing yet, am I?" she asked and then giggled. "Like I care. I know I'm only a few weeks along but I'm so excited I want to tell everyone. It's funny, all those years of being a model I always felt fat. Now I'm plump and I never felt better or looked more beautiful."

"It is a mystery," TJ joked and laughed. "You're

both beautiful." She smiled at Chloe. "I'm so happy for all of us."

Chloe nodded. It still felt like a dream.

"Sometimes you just know when something is right," Justin had said a few weeks after their second winter kiss. He was back out at the family ranch now running it along with his father. She'd been so glad to see how well they were getting along. They'd gotten a second chance and they both knew it.

"I know we're right together," he'd said.

She hadn't argued that. She'd never felt anything more strongly.

"Marry me." He'd gotten down on one knee. "Marry me, Chloe Clementine, and make me the happiest man alive."

What could she say? She smiled down into his handsome face. She loved this cowboy. "Yes. Oh yes."

When he'd slipped the ring on her finger, she'd begun to cry. They'd been through so much. Nothing could ever keep them apart again.

"How soon can we be married?" Justin had asked. "Maybe it's what we've been through, but I want to live every day to its fullest and not wait for anything I want this badly."

And here she was about to walk down the aisle with her sisters. Justin had loved the idea and so had she. It seemed right the three of them getting married together. Chloe just wished Grandma Frannie were here to see this.

She smiled at the thought. Frannie would have loved it. Chloe had the feeling that she knew and was pleased by how her girls had turned out.

A lot of things seemed right. Including the news that she was also pregnant. She wasn't ready to tell just yet. Justin was over the moon happy and his father was delighted he would be a grandfather.

Nici had stopped by the other day to tell her and Justin that she was going to community college in Miles City. "I don't know what I want to do with my life. I just know it's time I did something. Invite me to the wedding."

And they had.

Chloe took one last look in the mirror thinking she would wait to tell her sisters the good news she had to share about the baby. Just then Willie stuck her head in to fuss over her soon to be daughter-in-law, Annabelle, and to tell them that it was time. Her sisters crowded around her, all three of them smiling at each other in the mirror. TJ caught her eye and winked. There was no keeping anything a secret from sisters.

* * * * *

INTRIGUE

Available November 20, 2018

#1821 UNDERCOVER CONNECTION
by Heather Graham

FBI agent Jacob Wolff and Miami detective Jasmine Adair are frustrated when they discover they're both undercover to take down the same crime group. After their main informant is killed, can they find a way to work together to stop the ring before anyone else dies?

#1822 FIVE WAYS TO SURRENDER
Mission: Six • by Elle James

Navy SEAL Jake Schuler rescues Alexandria Parker, a teacher, from a group of terrorists in Niger. Will their teamwork be enough to save the other captives?

#1823 BULLETPROOF CHRISTMAS
Crisis: Cattle Barge • by Barb Han

Rory Scott returns to Cattle Barge on business, but his trip turns personal when he sees that Cadence Butler, a woman with whom he had an unforgettable fling, is pregnant. He will do anything to keep Cadence safe, especially since his unborn twins are in danger.

#1824 DELTA FORCE DADDY
Red, White and Built: Pumped Up • by Carol Ericson

Delta Force lieutenant Asher Knight has amnesia after a botched mission. When Paige Sterling claims she's his fiancée, he starts questioning everything around him, including whether the doctors at the rehabilitation center are helping him recover—or keeping him from remembering his past.

#1825 RENEGADE PROTECTOR
by Nico Rosso

Someone will do anything to get Mariana Balducci to sell her family orchard. Ty Morrison, a San Francisco cop and a member of a secret organization known as Frontier Justice, is Mariana's only hope...if she can trust him.

#1826 WYOMING CHRISTMAS RANSOM
Carsons & Delaneys • by Nicole Helm

Coroner Gracie Delaney has never believed Will Cooper's theory that the car accident that killed his wife two years ago was actually a murder. When Will's car is tampered with, causing a near-fatal crash, Gracie must accept that Will may be right. If so, a seasoned killer is now targeting Will.

An absolute melee had begun.

Jasmine helped up a young man, a white-faced rising star in a new television series. He tried to thank her.

"Get out, go—walk quickly," she said.

There were no more gunshots. But would they begin again?

She made her way to Josef Smirnoff, ducking beneath the notice of his distracted bodyguards. She knelt by him as people raced around her. "Josef?" she said, reaching for his shoulder, turning him over.

Blood covered his chest. Covered him. There was no hope for the man; he was already dead, his eyes open in shock. There was blood on her now, blood on the designer gown she'd been wearing, everywhere.

She looked up; Jorge had to be somewhere nearby.

That's when she knew she was about to be attacked herself.

There was a man coming after her, reaching for her.

She rolled quickly, avoiding him once. But as she prepared to fight back, she felt as if she had been taken down by a linebacker. She stared up into the eyes of the shaggy-haired newcomer. Bright blue eyes, startling against his face and dark hair. She felt his hands on her, felt the strength in his hold.

No. She was going to take him down.

She jack-knifed her body, letting him use his own weight against himself, causing him to crash into the floor.

He was obviously surprised; it took him a second—but only a second—to spin himself. He was back on his feet in a hunched position, ready to spring at her.

Where the hell was Jorge?

She feinted, as if she would dive down to the left, dove to the right instead, and caught the man with a hard chop to the abdomen that should have stolen his breath.

He didn't give; she was suddenly tackled again, down on the ground, feeling the full power of the man's strength atop her. She stared up into his eyes, blue eyes, glistening ice at the moment.

She realized the crowd was gone; she could hear the bustle at the doorway, hear the police as they poured in at the entrance.

But right there, at that moment Josef Smirnoff lay dead in an ungodly pool of blood—blood she wore—just feet away.

And there was this man.

And herself.

"Hey!" Thank God, Jorge had found her.

He dove down beside them, as if joining the fight.

But he didn't help Jasmine; he made no move against the man. He lay by Jasmine, as if he'd just been floored himself.

He whispered urgently, "Stop! FBI, meet MDPD. Jasmine, he's undercover. Jacob… Jasmine is a cop. My partner."

The man couldn't have looked more surprised. Then he made a play of socking Jorge, and Jorge lay still.

Jacob stood and dragged Jasmine to her feet. For a long moment he looked into her eyes, and then he wrenched her elbow behind her back.

"Play it out," he said, "nothing else to do."

"Sure," Jasmine told him.

And as he led her out—toward Victor Kozak, who now stood in the front, ready to take charge, Jasmine managed to twist and deliver a hard right to his jaw.

He swirled her around again, staring at her, and rubbing his jaw with his free hand.

"Play it out," she said softly.

Don't miss
Undercover Connection
by New York Times *bestselling author Heather Graham,
available November 20, 2018, wherever
Harlequin® Intrigue books and ebooks are sold.*

www.Harlequin.com

Ashley Jo "AJ" Somerfield couldn't help herself. She kept looking
out the window of the Stagecoach Saloon hoping to see a familiar
ranch pickup. Cyrus Cahill had promised to stop by as soon as he
returned to Gilt Edge. He'd been gone for over a week now after
going down to Denver to see about buying a bull for the ranch.

"I'll be back on Saturday," he'd said when he left. "Isn't that the
day Billie Dee makes chicken and dumplings?"

He knew darned well it was. "*Texas* chicken and dumplings,"
AJ had corrected him since everything Billie Dee cooked had
a little of her Southern spice in it. "I know you can't resist her
cookin', so I guess I'll see you then."

He'd laughed. Oh, how she loved that laugh. "Maybe you will
if you just happen to be tending bar on Saturday."

"I will be." That was something else he knew darned well.

He'd let out a whistle. "Then I guess I'll see you then."

She smiled to herself at the memory. It had taken Cyrus a while
to come out of his shell. One of those "aw shucks, ma'am" kind
of cowboys, he was so darned shy she thought she was going to
have to throw herself on the floor at his boots for him to notice her.
But once he had opened up a little, they'd started talking, joking
around, getting to know each other.

Before he went out of town, they'd gone for a horseback
ride through the autumn fallen leaves of the foothills up into the
towering pines of the forest. It had been Cyrus's idea. They'd
ridden up into one of the four mountain ranges that surrounded the
town of Gilt Edge—and the Cahill Ranch.

It was when they'd stopped to admire the view from the mountaintop that overlooked the small western town that AJ had hoped Cyrus would kiss her. He sure looked as if he'd wanted to as they'd walked their horses to the edge of the overlook.

The sun warming them while the breeze whispered through the boughs of the nearby pine trees, it was one of those priceless Montana fall days before the weather turned and winter blew in. That was why Cyrus had said they should take advantage of the beautiful day before he left for Denver.

Standing on the edge of the mountain, he'd reached over and taken her hand in his. "Beautiful," he'd said. For a moment she thought he was talking about the view, but when she met his gaze she'd seen that he meant her.

Her heart had begun to pound. This was it. This was what she'd been hoping for. He drew her closer. Pushing back his Stetson, he bent toward her. His mouth was just a breath away from hers—when his mare nudged him with her nose.

She could laugh about it now. But if she hadn't grabbed Cyrus, he would have fallen down the mountainside.

"She's just jealous," Cyrus had said of his horse as he'd rubbed the beast's neck after getting his footing under himself again.

But the moment had been lost. They'd saddled up and ridden back to Cahill Ranch.

AJ still wanted that kiss more than anything. Maybe today when Cyrus returned home. After all, it had been his idea to stop by the saloon his brother and sister owned when he got back. She thought it wasn't just Billie Dee's chicken and dumplings he was after and bit her lower lip in anticipation.

Find out if AJ gets that kiss in the exciting conclusion of The Montana Cahills series, available wherever HQN Books are sold November 2018.

www.Harlequin.com